M[] [] OF A

HUSTLER III:

REDEMPTION

An eye opening novel by
JABAR

Additional titles by <u>JABAR</u>:

Miseducation of a Hustler

Miseducation of a Hustler II: Educated Decisions

Good to the Last Drop

DEDICATIONS

This book is dedicated to the City of Kinloch, anyone who has ever called Kinloch home, and to those who tried to achieve success in the streets, lived well, laughed often and loved much; but who have not enjoyed the trust of good people, friends and family, the respect of intelligent women/men or the love of little children; who never fulfilled his/her dreams or accomplished much.

Although you may not have left the world better than you found it, fear not for it is not too late. By improving your way of thinking; appreciating the world's beauty; looking for the best in others and giving the world the best you have. Your life then will be an inspiration and your existence a memory and a true blessing.

In loving memory of Qualisha Mitchell
5/7/1987 – 8/23/2013

ACKNOWLEDGEMENTS

All praise due to God who continues to have mercy and grace on me.

To my children and Queen, I do it for you. My family and circle of close friends... I couldn't have done it without you, thank you.

To all of you who have supported my writing, blogged about my books and have requested more...I appreciate your support, thank you.

To write the Miseducation of a Hustler trilogy has been gratifying and a great honor. It allowed me to touch on myths and excuses often used for a moment, while seeing my words take the physical form of a book. If I could have but one wish, it would be for you to pass the positive messages along while demonstrating them yourself. After all, there is not much more to life than that.

Peace and God Bless
-JABAR

"It doesn't mater how much money you have, there's only two kinds of people: there's saved people and there's lost people ."

--Bob Dylan

MISEDUCATION OF A HUSTLER III: REDEMPTION

Printed in the United States

ISBN-13: 978-1502540690
ISBN-10: 150254069

Publisher's Note

CHAPTER ONE

Wisdom and those he consider family sat around his library discussing the events and how they unfolded while bringing Jamaal up to speed on things.

"I must be slow because I still haven't figured out how we pulled it off." Big Hands says totally confused.

"Might?" questioned Man-Man getting a laugh from everyone.

"Fuck yall, break it down for me Wisdom?" asked a truly confused Big Hands.

"No problem Big Hands. Limited Partner, Eagle Properties, FSK investors Black Investments and Edward Johnson Group invested more than $130.000,000 in un-built, unfinished, or properties lost in foreclosure but this was by design." Wisdom began to explain.

"We lost money on purpose?" asked Man-Man, he is now confused.

"That's the way it appeared. SEG is the acronym for Stone Equity Group, a Ronald Stone Company." said Wisdom, looking around with a big smile on his face while making sure everyone was following him.

"I still don't understand but go on." said Man-Man.

"Me either." said Jamaal.

"Hell none of us do." said Uncle Ronnie wanting Wisdom to get to the good part..

"Big Black had no idea that Dank managed SEG so as to defraud investors on purpose. The funds from limited partners and FSM investors were first deposited in an operating account for each particular investment but Dank and SEG as general partners immediately transferred all investor funds to a central SEG account. From there,

7

Dank personally controlled all expenditures, and SEG employees had standing instructions first to transfer 75% of what came into COG, then pay SEC's general operating expenses, and finally expenses for the various ongoing projects." Wisdom said stopping to make sure that everyone was following him.

"What is COG?" asked Hakim, this is the first time he'd ever heard of it.

"Cash Out Group." Dank answers for him with a big smile on his face.

"Go on." said Uncle Ronnie

"From January 2012 to July 2013, 582,500,000 was transferred to COG. Dank and I referred to the resulting shortfall, the difference between money on hand and money needed to replace project funds spent elsewhere, as the "black hole" As the black hole grew Dank and I took funds from new projects to complete old projects." Wisdom explained.

"Big Black never asked questions?'" ask Hakim.

"No, we were making money which built trust." Wisdom answers.

"So who lost all that money?" Big Hands asked.

"Big Black" Wisdom answered.

"So how does this play out?" asks Uncle Ronnie.

"Good question. Because we've siphoned off the majority of the funds, SEG went under and failed to make progress payments to Midwest Construction. There was no permanent financing coming, the result was devastating to Midwest Construction, leaving it unable to pay employees, subcontractors nor undertake new projects because its capital was tied up in the SEG projects." Wisdom explains.

"That's not all, we convinced Midwest Construction to extend their construction loans and wait while SEG looked for permanent financing." added Dank with a smile.

"You said there was no permanent financing coming." Big Hands says.

"There wasn't but we had to make him think that there was. You don't kick someone like Big Black, you crush him completely." said Wisdom.

"And after we accomplished that?" Hakim asks.

"We made sure that he had nowhere to run and no allies. This scheme also includes two different types of fraud on government agencies. First, SEG with Big Black's approval unbeknownst to him personally represented to the housing agencies that the National Development Council (NDC) was a nonprofit general partner in certain projects. In fact, NDC did not have a partnership agreement with SEG, and was unaware that SEG was using its name on tax credit applications. Based on those misrepresentations, nonprofit tax credits are allocated to SEG projects and ultimately claimed by their investors." said Wisdom.

"So the Feds were after him but the Panamanians got to him first?" asks Man-Man

"No, Rain reached out to his connect in Florida and found out who Brink's connect was and then tipped off Duke, greed made Duke want to take over." Wisdom explained.

"Damn, I didn't know Duke had it in him." said Dank surprised.

"Money is not the root of all evil, the want of it is." said Wisdom.

"The want?" asks Hakim.

"Yes, the want of money will make a person do crazy things. Add in the desire to have power and you have a recipe for disaster," said Wisdom.

"The St. Louis Evening Whirl described Big Black's office as a gun battle leaving three dead." injected Uncle Ronnie.

"I wish I could have seen how it went down." said Hakim who really wished that it was him gave Big Black what he deserved.

"Any questions?" asks Wisdom.

"Yea, what's the deal with Eagle Properties now?"Said Big Hands being that he and Man-Man were suppose to take it over,

"It was a throwaway company: we'll start a new one" Wisdom answers.

"And Silver Back Entertainment?" asks Dank.

"Our ownership will be transferred to Kinloch Organization for Uplifting African Americans (KOFUAA) the proceeds will be used to rebuild Kinloch." Wisdom answers proudly.

"What is KOFUAA?" Hakim asks.

"Have patience youngster, Uncle Ronnie will break it down to you real soon." Wisdom responds while grabbing Hakim around the neck.

"That's what I'm talking about?" said Jamaal happy that Wisdom hadn't forgotten about the things that they'd stayed up late at night in prison discussing.

"Okay then, what happens with all that money?" Hakim wanted to know.

"Redemption son, Redemption" replied Uncle Ronnie smiling at Wisdom proud of his grandson and his extended family.

"Now would you tell me what The Kinloch Organization for Uplifting African Americans is and why are we starting it" Hakim wanted to know.

"Yes, Hakim but you must first understand that we have been cruel, heartless, and callous in our rush to succeed and be great. Our selfish thoughts have been, let every man look out for himself; let every generation look out for itself, while we've fought against one another for scraps in the streets, that has to change. Uncle Ronnie do you mind further explaining." said Wisdom giving Uncle Ronnie the floor.

"Sure, I'll start with why. African Americans have become largely consumers indebted to other nationalities. Most African American communities remain economically underdeveloped, mired in poverty, and politically unstable. Realizing their common weaknesses, The Kinloch Organization for Uplifting African Americans is being established. The charter of the KOFUAA defines its aims as: promoting the unity of African Americans; eradicating all forms of colonialism; intensifying efforts to improve living standards; promoting cooperation; and defending the independence and sovereignty of all African Americans." said Uncle Ronnie proudly.

"So it's like the White Lotus Society or the Black Dragon Society? Dank asks now more interested than ever.

"No, it's more like the Society of American Indians except we're offering classes, business building skills, job training, and providing a home ownership program." Uncle Ronnie answers.

"I understand most of what you are saying but the home ownership program went over my head. I don't completely understanding how it will work." Man-Man says seeking clarification.

"Its rather simple, anyone enrolled in the program can earn up to $500 attending classes which in turn can only be used towards a down payment for one of the homes built by United Construction. But it's not that simple, they must then sign up for the Home Ownership Program that will further educate them on the process. Finally, their services will be required in building the homes which keeps cost down. We will offer newly built homes at the price it cost us to build them with a no interest abort term loan; however there will be some stipulations." Uncle Ronnie answers with a serious look on his face.

"What kind of stipulations?" Dank asks.

"Participants will be required sign a contract that will basically says that in the event that their home is kicked in and drugs are found, they loose the house, no exception! However, they won't loose everything, we will return the down payment, minus rent and damages if there are any." answered Uncle Ronnie.

"Please explain?" Man-Man requested.

"Say that a participant has put, down $5.000 on a house that cost us $75,000 to build. Their monthly payment would be around $1000 a month for 70 months. If they lived in the house 45 months, and then their house is kicked in and drugs are found. We would return the $5000 minus $500 for each month they stayed in the home for rent. If there's no damage to the property they would receive $29,000: $5,000 + 48 x $500 $29,000 and the house will go back into the program." Uncle Ronnie answers while looking around to make sure that everyone was following him.

"Is $1000 a month reasonable?" Jamaal questioned unsure if those they were trying to help could afford that much.

"Yes, nowadays people know the price of everything and the value of nothing. The real price, what it really costs a person who wants to acquire it, is the toil and trouble of acquiring it. They will appreciate what we're offering after completing the classes because they will understand that the delay of instant gratification is worth what will eventually gain from making the sacrifice." Wisdom quickly answers.

"So basically you are saying that they got to stop spending their money on bullshit and focus on the things that are really important?" Hakim asks.

"Exactly." replied Wisdom.

"That's cool but why us" asks Dank.

"We are meant to work together with others in the community and church. The Good Lord desires that we take part in fellowship while using our spiritual gifts and working together in his service. For various reasons, some aren't able to help themselves. Yet they are a needed part of the community. That's when others can meet their needs. We must do our part so that others may feel they're an integral part of the community. We work better together than alone." said Uncle Ronnie looking around the room,

"That's real talk." Jamaal agreed.

"Jamaal it seems you've become a lot more religious since going to prison. From what I've heard, you were a totally different person before you went in." Dank stated trying to get a better understanding of who Jamaal really is.

"I was a different person before going to prison. While incarcerated, during a conversation with my mother she said to me "Jamaal you've given the streets a chance, now why don't you give God one." That statement hit me like a ton of bricks because it was the truth, so I did. I didn't fall head first into it, little by little I began to study the word, and when I did, I began to see God working in other people lives as well as mine. Reading the Bible became exciting. Peter's story in the Book of Acts became just as thrilling as a movie; being miraculously released from his chains and walking past the sleeping soldiers on his way to freedom or the stories of Jesus raising the dead." Jamaal explained.

Dank has a skeptical look on his face.

"You don't really take that to mean, that Jesus was raising people from the dead literally, do you?" Dank asks while watching Jamaal closely.

"Without a doubt or contradiction, if a man can fall dead right here before us, we call the paramedics, they come, and hook him up to a man made machine and resuscitate him. Didn't they bring him back to life?" asked Jamaal locking eyes with Dank.

"Of course." said Dank.

"Then why couldn't Jesus?" ask Jamaal still looking at Dank waiting on a reply as everyone looked on.

"You make a valid point, I never looked at it that way." replied Dank who now looked at Jamaal in a different light.

CHAPTER TWO

Jamaal and Dank's conversation seems to have given everyone something to think about. Since knowing one another God had never entered into their conversation or their individual beliefs.

Wisdom was taken by surprise with Uncle Ronnie's comment about "The Good Lord". Growing up he'd never heard him speak about God nor did he take them to church. Nevertheless he was happy to know that Uncle Ronnie wasn't foolish enough to not believe in the Lord or praise him.

"Wisdom, I respect what you're saying and I'm riding with you but we're going to encounter some serious resistance on both sides." said Hakim snapping Wisdom out of his thoughts,

"Your observation is correct" Wisdom conceded.

"So what's the plan?" asked Man-Man who was down for whatever.

"First we need to educate the people, it'll make them easier to talk too, easier to assist and impossible to enslave." injected Uncle Ronnie.

"Education cost money." Dank reminded everyone.

"It does but ignorance cost everyone more!" Jamaal quickly replies while sitting up in his seat.

"We have the money and means, all we need is the right application of both." Wisdom said as he sat giving the situation some serious thought.

Our people want change and a better life, if we trust them, they will be true to us. If we treat them greatly, they will show themselves great." stated Uncle Ronnie believing every word,

"What about the guys hustling the block?" asked Big Hands knowing that dealing with them wouldn't be easy.

"When I was a teenager hanging out on Lyons St. hustling across the street from the church, I remember when ole boy came home from prison he was in the Moorish Science Temple. He started telling us we couldn't hustle over there. We spared him because we knew his entire family. Instead of murking him we want to his brother's and explained that he wasn't about to stop the hustle. His brother's got through to him; he would come by and look but never said anything else. We were young, ignorant, didn't give a fuck, and was dead serious, this his brother's knew. Those guys are no different said Wisdom not sleeping on the streets.

"So what do we do?" asked Jamaal knowing that there had to be a solution.

"First we provide opportunities for those who want them." Wisdom suggested.

"And for those who don't take the carrot, they get the stick?" asked Man-Man who doesn't have a problem reaching an understanding with anyone that got in the way of progress.

"No, we can't go around murking brothers just because they are ignorant, we used to be them." Wisdom emphasized.

"Then what other options do we have available to us?" Dank asks knowing that this wasn't going to be an ease task.

"We studied history which has taught us that the mass controls. If we educate and provide opportunities for the people, they will demand that these activities stop or be moved to the out skirts. Not with violence but by not condoning or accepting the behavior." Uncle Ronnie answers.

"Some will resist!" said Hakim making sure this point wasn't overlooked,

"Sure but we anticipate that; however, a vicious dog will retreat if he sees 50 cats standing their ground." said Uncle Ronnie making sure that everyone understood that as a unit they could do anything.

"Are you saying this can be accomplished without violence?" asked Big Hands making sure he understood them correctly.

"I can't guarantee that on their part but it's our goal to achieve success without the use of any. But don't get it twisted the happiness and safety of the multitude will not be forfeited by the selfish desires of a few. We've all been in the game and know the rules." Wisdom says with a vicious look on his face and letting his words hang in the air.

"No doubt, get out of line, you get whacked." added Hakim.

"Now, I'm confused, I thought you said we weren't going to murk anyone." Jamaal says looking at Wisdom.

"We're not, as we all know whacked has more then one meaning i.e. being broken financially, mentally or being in prison just to name a few. Were not goons or cavemen, our way of doing things will be diplomatic." Uncle Ronnie assured everyone.

"Look at it this way. The United States told Saddam Hussein to stop oppressing his people and building weapons of mass destruction. When talks didn't work they offered him silver i.e. retire with your money and move on." Wisdom said trying to see if they were following him.

"But they murdered him." stated Big Hands not getting Wisdom's point.

"No, he forced their hand choosing hot lead instead" Uncle Ronnie explained.

"We're not trying to stop the hustle, that's the job of the police; however, we want to move it to the out skirts so that the hood is a safer place." Wisdom said.

"So we create a Red Light District?" asked Big Hands.

"HELL NO, we're not becoming co-conspirators in anything, we simply plant a seed, leaving them a way out"' stated Wisdom making sure his words weren't falling on deaf ears.

"Those guys aren't going to be easy to talk too." said Jamaal dreading an encounter with them.

"Probably not but we can't watch with hands off on this one, we must try." stated Wisdom.

"And if that doesn't work?" asked Hakim.

"Then we'll speak a language they WILL understand!" stated Uncle Ronnie sitting back in his chair.

"What about those in power, the City Officials?" Dank asks knowing that they were the true puppet masters.

"All of them need to go" Man-Man spat, disgusted with how the hood has been run down.

"Some of them are being prohibited from doing what is good for the community." offered Uncle Ronnie.

"We must think this through. Only idiots fix what's not broken or implement change for change's sake without retaining the strength of the previous organization." said Jamaal making sure that their emotions didn't get in the way of progress.

"You're correct; our success is rooted in simplicity, we get rid of the bad apples and keep the good ones." stated Wisdom.

For the next couple of hours they sat around discussing the best way to implement their plan. Nothing would come easy, this everyone was in agreement with; however, nothing in life worth having ever does.

"I like this plan." said Dank ready to get started.

"Good. Now I want to congratulate Jamaal." Announced Uncle Ronnie

"Thanks Uncle Ronnie." Replied Jamaal happy he had everyone's support

"Don't let the title President and CEO go to your head." said Man-Man jokingly.

"Never, KOFUAA is about uplifting the people; I'm just an instrument being used for the cause." Jamaal says with pride.

"We need all hands on deck for getting this organization off the ground, this includes teaching workshops." said Wisdom looking around at everyone making sure that they understood him.

"What am I going to teach?" asked Big Hands feeling like teaching was out of reach for him.

"Along with Uncle Ronnie you could teach self-defense classes or work with Man-Man on workout programs" answered Wisdom.

"I never thought about that." Replied Big Hands not feeling left out anymore.

"From being in prison we know that the mental needs to be on one accord with the spiritual; and the physical." said Jamaal.

"I agree." says Uncle Ronnie.

"We all bring something unique to the table that others can benefit from which makes for a great team. A lot of people get caught up on being the captain of the ship instead of being content with being on it. There has been times throughout our relationship were the leadership role has changed depending on the task. Being a good leader requires knowing when to fall back allowing someone else with the needed skills to lead while you aid and assist the team" said Wisdom

"Spoke like a true team player." said Dank with a smile.

CHAPTER THREE

Sky and Uncle Ronnie incorporated United Construction as a C Corporation. Then sought and were accepted as a Minority Business Enterprise (MBE), Women Owned Business Enterprise (WBE), the Veterans Affairs (VA), and the SBA 8 (a) business development program. Having these affiliations evens the playing field when trying to obtain government contracts,

KOFUAA, is currently housed temporally in the old Kinloch High School which would have to do for now; however they knew that a state of the art facility needed to be built in order to achieve their goals.

Over the past month Sky, Jamaal and Uncle Ronnie spent countless hours with land surveyors and architects working out the kinks in their plan. Properly constructing homes while buildings them to block out the sounds of airplanes is one of their major concerns. Also important is preserving the old world charm which they wouldn't ignore; the thought of building clusters of cookie cutter homes and buildings wasn't what they envisioned.

United Construction requested and was granted a meeting with Kinloch City Officials on their proposal. Sky, Uncle Ronnie and Jamaal met with Scott Snow, a public official, Jason Washington, the Deputy Mayor, and Mayor Oscar Brown at the City Hall to discuss their plans.

"Thank you for seeing us." said Sky shaking each of their hands before taking her seat.

"Our pleasure, I understand that you have a desire to build in the City of Kinloch?" Mayor Brown asks with a friendly smile.

"That is correct; we have a desired to rebuild this community while providing much needed opportunities for the residents." Sky explains.

"What do those plans consist of?" Mayor Brown asks moving the meeting along.

"Our plan is to rebuild the City of Kinloch in three phases: The first phase begins with a state of the art facility to house, The Kinloch Organization for Uplifting African Americans as known as (KOFUAA). This establishment offers a multitude of classes and skilled trades." Sky informed them.

"And phase two?" the Mayor questions.

"In phase two our goal is to build a business incubator along with a business district providing business opportunities and jobs." Sky answered.

"And phase three?" the Mayor inquired.

"Our goal is to build 200 homes, a condominium development, 2 schools, and a grocery store." answered Sky.

"Your plans are very ambitious and will cost millions of dollars. The tax payers can't afford to foot the bill." Mayor Brown states as he watches Sky closely.

"They are but they are nothing that we can't handle including the cost." Sky emphasized.

"Is the area zoned for their proposed development?" Mayor Brown asks, turning to look at the Deputy Mayor.

"Sir, they would need to obtain numerous approvals from various city agencies in order to proceed with the developments." answered Deputy Mayor Washington.

"We all share common goals, approval shouldn't be

an issue" said Uncle Ronnie not understanding why there would be any complications.

"Approvals are not that simple, there are procedures and protocols that must be followed." said Mayor Brown.

"We understand that's why we've hired the best architects and consultants to draft out plans to meet code." said Sky handing a copy of their plans to the Mayor and one to his staff.

After quickly glancing over the plans Mayor Brown was now ready to make his ruling.

"I like your idea; however, at this time I must deny your request." Stated Mayor Brown standing indicating that the meeting is over.

"That's it? Sky says standing wanting an explanation.

"This is some bullshit." yelled Uncle Ronnie standing.

Jamaal quickly grabbed his arm.

"Calm down." Jamaal whispers to Uncle Ronnie, although he feels the same way.

"There's nothing I can do for you at this time, have a nice day." Said Mayor Brown and then he hastily exits the room.

Quickly gathering their things, Sky, Uncle Ronnie and Jamaal made their way to the door devastated and disappointed. Never did they imagine the meeting ending with them being denied.

They had assumed everyone would be ecstatic to see the City of Kinloch rise from the ashes, an assumption they were dead wrong about.

Deputy Mayor Washington caught up with Jamaal

before he had a chance to get into his car.

"Jamaal, let me speak to you for a moment." requested Deputy Mayor Washington pulling him to the side.

"What's up?" asked Jamaal trying not to show his contempt for the man.

"I suggest you speak with Scott Snow, and Tyrone Price, they are political consultant to facilitate meetings between yourself and Mayor Brown." said Deputy Mayor Washington trying to read Jamaal.

"We just had a meeting and were rejected, did you not hear him?" Jamaal says in a tone that spooks the Deputy Mayor.

"Calm down, you're correct, the three of you had an official meeting: but you will have a private one. No, doesn't always mean no forever." stated Deputy Mayor Washington hoping that he didn't have to spell it out for Jamaal.

"How much of a bribe will it take? Asks Jamaal who hated dealing with criminals disguised as upstanding citizens.

"Bribe is a very nasty work, please never use it again. A donation is all that we ask." utters Deputy Mayor Washington.

Jamaal stood listening to Deputy Mayor Washington describe how he could bribe Mayor Brown to expedite the real estate development, all the while despising the man even more.

"How does that sound?" asks the Deputy Mayor when he finished explaining.

"How much?" Jamaal questioned.

"I will facilitate meetings between you, Mayor

Brown, Snow, and Price; in exchange for $25,000. The money should be broken up into smaller increments to conceal the identity of the real contributor." Deputy Mayor Washington informed him.

"You'll have the money within 24 hours, make it happen." stated Jamaal before walking away.

Driving to United Construction, Jamaal had the urge to turn around, go back and flat line all the crooked bastards. Instead he pulled into the old Eagle Properties parking lot, now United Construction where everyone is waiting on him to return.

"What took you so long?" asked Dank as Jamaal entered the door.

"I'll tell you when everyone is gathered around." Jamaal replies while trying to keep himself composed.

"Hey, everyone Jamaal needs all of our attention." yelled Dank.

Once everyone was in the room, Jamaal explained his encounter with Deputy Mayor Washington as everyone listened on, some in total disbelief.

"Those greedy bastards" yelled Hakim pounding his fist on the table.

"Calm down, Hakim, we must think this through with level heads" Wisdom reminds him,

"I've seen this before, if we pay, they'll continue to squeeze us." Janet warns everyone.

"She's right." Agreed Pam.

"So what do we do?" asked Man-Man.

"We have the money, it won't hurt us" said Jamaal not knowing what else to do.

"Money isn't the issue, I don't like being pressed." said Wisdom as his wheels began to spin.

"Me either" says Big Hands.

"I can find out where they sleep." suggested Hakim.

"We can't do that Hakim. In contrast to revenge, the natural reaction to transgressions, which, can be expected and even calculated, the act of forgiving can never be predicted; it is the only reaction that acts in an unexpected way retaining something of the original spirit of the action." stated Jamaal looking at Hakim.

"We going to forgive them and they are fucking over our people, is that what you're saying?" asked Hakim not feeling Jamaal.

"Yes, Jamaal is right. There are other factors you have failed to consider. Hakim, I told you to spend more time studying history." said Wisdom disappointed at Hakim's first impulse on handling the situation.

"What does history have to do with it?" asked Hakim feeling like the greedy bastards should get what their hand called for.

"Everything! If you recall The Commission which consisted of the top Mafia Dons had a meeting because Albert Anastasia, a Boss, who ran Murder Inc., wanted to whack a top District Attorney which obviously would have been bad for business." said Wisdom making sure that Hakim was following him.

"Go on" Hakim says.

"The Commission tried to explain to Anastasia how the government would bring their full force down on their organization if this was to happen. Anastasia, a hot head

27

stormed out of the meeting determined to do things his way. When he left, another meeting was held..." Wisdom, was saying before Uncle Ronnie cut him off,

"That's enough Wisdom, Hakim's not ignorant, he can read between the lines." stated Uncle Ronnie.
Hakim looks at Wisdom knowing that he is right.

"Okay, it was a bad idea. What do we do?" asked Hakim.

"I'll go see Brinks, he will know how to handle this or know someone who does." said Wisdom.

"That sounds like a good idea. Brinks and Rain will came up with something." said Man-Man knowing that with Brinks and Rain's experience they would be able to navigate these un-chartered waters.

The group sat around into the wee hours of the night debating and discussing their different ideas until they had a solid plan. Paying Deputy Mayor Washington $23,700 wouldn't be a problem for the time being everyone agreed and would buy them some much needed time.

CHAPTER FOUR

Deputy Mayor Washington made an unexpected visit to KOFUAA finding Jamaal preparing for his first class.

KNOCK, KNOCK, he tapped on the door causing Jamaal to look up.

"Come in." said Jamaal surprised to see him.

"I like what you've done with the place." said Deputy Mayor Washington stepping into his office.

"Thank you."

"The sign out front is a bit dramatic isn't it?" the Deputy Mayor asks.

"No, I want it to be clear that trespassers who have ill will of KOFUAA will be shot and if the survive they will be shot again."

"Now, now I like the sign hanging over your head." the Deputy Mayor says as he steps closer to look at it.

"Follow me if I advance, kill me if I retreat, avenge me if I die fighting, are words that I live by. I had intentions on seeing you later." said Jamaal hoping that the Deputy Major caught his drift as he reaches into his desk retrieving a large manila envelope.

"Whoa" exclaimed Deputy Mayor Washington.

"What's wrong?" asked Jamaal

"Nothing our agreement is still intact, you have our full cooperation; however, I don't deal in cash. Jamaal, Missouri law requires a campaign to identify contributions exceeding $300, the campaign donor's name, address, occupation, employer, and employer's occupation in the periodic reports the campaign files with the Missouri Election Law Enforcement Commission." explained Deputy Mayor Washington.

"I didn't know that." said Jamaal

"Try spreading the contributions among different campaign and political committees benefiting Mayor Brown's campaign, such as the upcoming political fundraiser "Kinloch Day" which is sponsored by the Kinloch Democratic Committee for Brown's benefit. I'm the Executive Producer of the event. Lastly, obtain specifications for the Development, which I will discuss with a high-level zoning official. This is very important and will open doors." Deputy Mayor Washington says.

"I'll handle it." Jamaal assures him.

"Also I'm not sure if you are aware but I'm a real estate broker. Being United Construction's exclusive broker selling units in the condominium development would be appreciated." said Deputy Mayor Washington with a smile.

"No problem. We are 100% ready to do some things with your help and your assistance." said Jamaal standing to show Deputy Mayor Washington to the door.

"Good, good, this is the beginning of something wonderful." assured Deputy Mayor Washington shaking Jamaal's hand before leaving.

"Greedy. Slimy motherfucker," Jamaal says to himself as he heads into the restroom to wash his hands. Returning, he put the money away, grabs his briefcase, locked his door and heads for his first class; the campaign contributions would have to wait until later.
Entering the classroom Jamaal is happy to see that he has a full class in attendance.

"Good morning class. My name is Jamaal Burns, you can call me Jamaal. Welcome to Building a Solid Foundation." said Jamaal as he scans the room.

After making proper introduction learning everyone's name, Jamaal begins to explain the purpose of the class.

"In this class you will learn how to become financially literate. This will allow you to make your money work for you so that you don't have to work for money. Understanding this concept will provide you with financial freedom." Jamaal explained while looking around the class.

"We don't even have jobs." Shawn points out the obvious.

"Who said anything about a job? Having a job doesn't assure you anything. Have you heard of the 80/20 Rule?" Jamaal asked him.

"No, what is that?" Shawn replies

"Life is 20 percent of that happens to you and 80 percent of what you make of it." answered Jamaal

"Meaning what?" Asked Shawn

"It means that the only thing you have control over in your life is how you respond." Jamaal answered looking directly at Shawn.

"It's not easy to respond positive when bad things are constantly happening to you." Stated Shawn feeling like Jamaal just didn't understand.

"Be thankful anyway." Jamaal uttered

"Be thankful, are you crazy?" asked Shawn not feeling Jamaal.

"Yes, in everything give thanks, for everything

you are going through or have been through for having been through it is the will of God." Jamaal told him.

"Man I didn't sign up for church." Said Shawn now becoming upset and standing to leave.

"Please be seated. I'm not a preacher, nor am I here to tell you bad things won't happen. I'm here to help you deal with them." Jamaal informs him

"So you saying that God let bad things happen? Asked Shawn trying to get a better understanding.

"What I'm saying is Jesus didn't promise to change the circumstances around us, but he did promise great peace and pure joy to those who would learn to believe that God actually controls all things. The very act of praise releases the power of God into a set of circumstances and enables God to change them if this is his design." Jamaal answered.

"That didn't answer my question" stated Shawn

"You are not hearing me because your heart is blocking what I'm saying to you. Very often it is our attitudes that hinders the solution to a problem. God is the supreme ruler and could certainly cut across out wrong thought patterns and attitudes. But his perfect plan is to bring us into fellowship and communion with him, and so he allows circumstances and incidents which will bring our wrong attitudes to our attention." Jamaal educates him

"No matter what we do?' asked Shawn

"Don't think of your past as a chain around your neck. Thank God for every detail of your life and believe He has permitted all of these

32

things in order to bring you to the place where you are now. And that doesn't just mean things that happen after you've asked God to take over your life, God is able to use even our past." said Jamaal now looking around the room.

Satisfied with Jamaal's answer, Shawn takes his seat as Jamaal begins the lesson he has planned for the day.

"Do you know the difference between an asset and a liability?' Jamaal asks pointing at Christy.

"Yes my assets are my car and house. My liabilities are credit card bills etc." Christy quickly replies

"Not exactly, simply put assets are anything that puts money into your pocket; liabilities are anything that takes money out. There are good assets and bad assets as well as good and bad liabilities; we'll get to those in a moment. Your house in not an assets technically because you must pay a mortgage, taxes, insurance, and maintenance. On the banks financial statement your house is listed as an asset because you pay them a mortgage every month (money leaving your pocket), the same is true for your car." said Jamaal

"So when does my house become an asset?" asked Christy curious.

"If your mortgage is paid off and the combined cost of your taxes, insurance, and maintenance is less then 20% of your monthly income then it becomes an asset and a good liability." answered Jamaal.

"What is a good liability?" asked Jackie

"Say for instance you borrow money to start a business that generates money which allows you to pay off the loan, then the loan is a good liability. Also a car is needed for transportation and a home to live in; however, it's the cost of the car or house we choose versus our income that makes that determination" Jamaal told her.

"So how does a person buy a house in a really nice neighborhood if he doesn't have all cash?" John asks.

"First as a community we can make any community nice if we do so as a collective unit. This is what we should strive for instead of running away," answered Jamaal..

"I feel you." replied John.

"However to answer your question, if it is your desire to live in a neighborhood you can't afford, I would recommend that you pyramid your way into the house of your dreams." Jamaal answered.

"Huh?" asked John

"Other cultures will live 20 people in a three bedroom house splitting the bills. In 10 months saving their money each family has enough to buy a starter house for say $40,000 that needs some work. They buy the house paying cash then work to improve it; over the next two years investing $15,000-$20,000 on repairs doing most of the work themselves. In two years the house is now worth $95,000 when they sell the house they take advantage of *IRS Code* 1031. The 1031 exchange, sometimes called Starker Exchanges, allows for the postponement of capital gains tax payment when one property is sold and another property of like kind is purchased within a specified time period. The IRS has defined like kind as any property held for business, trade, or investment purposes. That generous interpretation means that you can use a 1031 exchange when you sell your investment multifamily house and use the profit to buy a gas station/convenience store, and vice versa." Jamaal explained,

"Wow, why don't more people do this?" asked Jackie.

"Most people don't know and for those who do, they lack the discipline." answered Jamaal

"So I could take the $95,000 and buy $250,000 house?" asked Christy.

"Yes and if you are smart, you will buy a $250,000 in a good neighborhood that hasn't been cared for. This will allow you to purchase it for say $170,000. After putting another say $40,000 into it in mostly do-it-yourself improvements, you've gained at least $40,000 in equity. And even if you had to get a 30 year mortgage for the $75,000 at a high 6% interest rate you would only have to pay $449.66 a month. Rates are now at an all time low, under 4.0% so at 4.1% the payments would be $362.40." Jamaal informed her.

"So when we see the interest rate advertised on television as 3.3% it doesn't apply to everyone?" asked Jackie

"No it doesn't, you must remember that your interest rate will depend on your credit score. The higher your score, the lower your interest rate will be." answered Jamaal

"Why does someone have a low credit score?" asked Jackie

"Because you are bad about paying people," Shawn yells out which got a laugh out of everyone.

"That's not necessarily true. People falsely assume they have good credit because they've never used it, their wrong. It takes debt to have a good credit score. Having good credit doesn't mean having no debts: To show that you are a good credit customer, you have to show that you can manage credit." stated Jamaal

"What's wrong with using credit?" ask Tina.

"A person who is in debt is a slave to the creditor. If you look back at the early 1920 and 30's most people bought what they could afford which allowed them to live better stress free lives. Today we are told that credit is good and that we should strive to have good credit. That's some bullshit." stated Jamaal

"So having good credit is bad?" asked Tina not clearly understanding him.

"I'm not saying that but consider the following, who in their right mind strives to be in debt? Why would you want to owe someone when you don't have too? Why would you agree to pay someone for 30 years, when you can simply discipline yourself delaying instant gratification until you can afford it?" asked Jamaal.

"But everyone says that we need good credit in this world" Said Tina.

"That's because those who hold the gold and make the rules have fed society that line of bullshit. Look at the Mormans, Amish and Jews, they own and control because they have great self-discipline and benefit from those who don't. Said Jamaal

"Ok, I understand now, I guess you have a point." said Tina.

"No disrespect but I'm simply trying to get you all to understand that when you accept credit, they become the pimp and you become the hoe. Rain, sleet or snow, they expect you to hit that track and get their money." said Jamaal explained in a way that they could relate to.

"I never looked at it that way, I'm not being pimped by nobody." stated Tina.

"I would hope not." replied Jamaal.

"I think I am going to like this class." said Shawn taking notes.

"Class, our time is up for today. I would like to thank all of you for stepping outside of your comfort zone to attend this class. If you enjoyed my class, I can assure you that all of the other classes that you have signed up for will be just as informative or better, have a great day." said Jamaal dismissing the class.

Ending his first class Jamaal felt like he had gotten through to them. Loading his things back into his briefcase, he was happy to look up and see Hakim.

"Professor how was class?" asked Hakim making fun of him.

"Great, the class went really well." Jamaal informed Hakim.

"How can I help?" asked Hakim.

Opening back up his briefcase, Jamaal removed a binder handing it to Hakim.

"What is this?" asked Hakim looking at it like it was a snake.

"It's a coupon organizer. The coupons are separated by categories such as foods, stores, and supplies." Jamaal informed him.

"What do you want me to do with it?" asked Hakim confused.

"Get someone to help you then log onto doublesavingdivas.com, thefrugalgirls.com and/or commonsensewithmoney.com for the latest deals and coupons." said Jamaal.

"You seriously want me to go couponing?" asked Hakim looking at Jamaal like he had lost his mind.

"Yes, the school and the food banks need to stay

stocked. And don't try to cut corners, you will teach a class on this." said Jamaal before walking away.

"How did I go from being a gangster to couponing?" hakim asked himself looking at the binder.

CHAPTER FIVE

Pulling up to The Walls brought back old memories for Wisdom. He hadn't been back to the prison since his release although he made sure that Sky and Justice visited his father often.

It wasn't that he didn't want to see his father, he really missed the conversations they shared but prison was a place that he was allergic too.

Stepping out of the truck, Wisdom made his way to the line of waiting visitors. Seeing so many women standing three dedicated to making the long trip was something he admired.

He listened as visitors spoke about how unpleasant the process was. For him it was nothing in contrast to the humiliating strip searches inmates must endure before being allowed to enter the visiting room the thought alone angered him.

The line moved slowly by design, guards wanted inmate to get as little visiting time as possible. Some thought it was their job to further punish inmates every chance they got. Finally, Wisdom made it to the visitor registration counter.

"Who are you here to visit? Asked the guard while accepting his State ID.

"Kareem Smith." replied Wisdom.

After typing several things into the computer, Wisdom was allowed to enter the visiting room. The place felt like a funeral home, he though approaching the guards station.

"Who are you here to visit? Asked a female guard.

"Kareem Smith." Replied Wisdom thinking that this process was redundant.

"Table 11, the rules are on the table." She said as he walked off.

While waiting, Wisdom decided to grab his father some items from the vending machine. Knowing that his was secretly on a health kick, he grabbed him a salad, orange juice, trail mix, some cashews and a cappuccino for himself.

Returning to the table he sat the items down and took his seat. Looking around he spotted several guys he knew from inside, returning each of their nods.

Wisdom sat thinking to himself about how that was him on the other side of the table not too long ago, a thought that he didn't enjoy. Brinks finally made his way into the visiting room after what seemed like forever.

"You don't look too happy to see me!" stated Wisdom with a smile standing to embrace his father.

"Always, I was expecting Sky and Justice but you will have to do. To what do I owe this pleasure?" he asked as he embraced his son, and then taking his seat.

"We need to talk but there is no rush. How have you been? Asked Wisdom.

"Blessed considering my present circumstance and you? Asked Brinks.

"Too blessed to be depressed." replied Wisdom taking a sip of Cappuccino.

"You didn't come all this way for small talk, spill it," ordered Brinks.

"Several politicians are hindering our plans to

rebuild." Wisdom told him.

"Tell me about it." replied Brinks removing the top from his salad.

Wisdom began explaining to his father everything that had occurred and how he'd sat down with everyone to come up with a solution.

"Interesting but there are more player's." said Brinks tossing a handful of cashews into his mouth.

"Why do you say that?" asked Wisdom.

"Total control is never given to people like Mayor Brown and his cronies." Brinks answered.

"How then are they able to do what they do?" asked Wisdom

"This I don't know but I know someone who can find out for me." said Brinks.

"That would really help." replied Wisdom now looking at things from a different angle.

"So what is your plan?" asked Brinks.

"I have a general idea but I can't properly construct one without more information." answered Wisdom truthfully.

"Give me a couple of weeks to do some research, if you don't have time to come back, send Sky." said Brinks.

"That sounds good, thanks." Wisdom replied now feeling much better.

"So how is my granddaughter doing?" asked Brinks changing the subject.

"Great, she wants a brother or sister." Wisdom answered.

"What's wrong with that?" asked Brinks observing his sons reaction.

"Nothing, I think Sky wants another baby

too." said Wisdom.

"And you?" asks Brinks eyeing his son,

"I don't have a problem with it." Wisdom answered.

"So what's the hold up?" asked his father.

"I'm just trying to get things in order first." said Wisdom.

"Ha-ha, good luck" said Brinks laughing.

"What's so funny?" asks Wisdom not getting the joke.

"Things will never be perfect. When you put out one fire, another one will pop up. That's called life." Brinks inform his son.

"You're right." replied Wisdom knowing that it was the truth.

"Rain has a parole date." stated Brinks while opening up the trail mix.

"When?" asked Wisdom happy to hear about Rain's blessing.

"I assume soon." replied Brinks tossing a handful of the trail mix into his mouth.

"You don't know?" asked Wisdom surprised.

"He didn't tell me but I can tell." Brinks answers.

"Why wouldn't he tell you?" asked Wisdom thinking this was out of character for Rain.

"I'm assume it has something to do with the brothers of guy who he killed." Brinks speculates.

"Rain wasn't the aggressor besides he doesn't appear to be the scared type." said Wisdom.

"Your observation is on point. He just doesn't want anything to spill over into the positive things that you all are doing." said Brinks.

"I understand that but he's family. It would be wise for the brothers to stand-down." said Wisdom knowing that they really didn't want it with them.

"I know we have a hands-off policy when it comes to family and I fully support it but Rain is very smart and crafty, don't worry about him, just be there in case he needs you." said Brinks.

"His transition will be smooth, believe that." assured Wisdom as his wheels starting to spin.

"Also, you know I have less than 8 years left on my sentence. My custody level will drop making me eligible for a transfer to a lower level prison. I'm not feeling that." stated Brinks waiting to see Wisdom's reaction.

"I know you're comfortable here but you need to be at a lower level prison." said Wisdom understanding his father's reasons but knowing that transitioning out was important.

"I'll give it some thought." replied Brinks.

"You already have or you wouldn't have brought it up. You'll be closer to home so you will get to see Justice more." said Wisdom.

"So you gone play that card on me?" asked Brinks with a smile.

"Just stating the facts, she loves seeing you." said Wisdom.

"That's my baby, I'd do anything for her." said Brinks with a big smile.

"Then its settled." stated Wisdom enjoying the small victory.

"It is." said his father with a smile.

"VISITS ARE NOW OVER" came blaring a loud voice over the visiting room speakers.

"Damn, time went by so fast.. Thanks for coming, I needed this." said Brinks standing to embrace his son.

"Anytime, so did I." said Wisdom standing preparing to do the same.

"Don't put so much time in-between the next one." said his father hugging him.

"I won't." Wisdom assured his father; however, he was thinking that he had to get him out of that cage soon.

The feeling that Wisdom had watching his father walkway was a feeling that he had never experienced; one of genuine love and respect. Walking out of the prison, stepping back into his truck, Wisdom knew that this fight wouldn't be easy or unavoidable.

CHAPTER SIX

After dressing out Brinks returned to three house going directly to Banker Bob's cell.

"Got a minute?' asked Brinks causing Banker Bob to look up from the Wall Street Journal he is reading.

"Always for a friend." he replies setting down the paper he was reading.

"I have a problem that requires your expertise." said Brinks not stroking his ego but letting him know that this was something out of his area of expertise.

Brinks spent the next thirty minutes explaining only the needed to know details to Banker Bob, in hopes that he would have a quick solution while realizing that he was most likely wishful thinking.

"There's a Whale lurking." stated Banker Bob once Brinks had finished telling him everything.

"What do you mean? asked Brinks confused.

"I mean there's someone bigger who's behind this. Building something like you're proposing requires approval from some higher up officials and cost millions of dollars." explained Banker Bob.

"A Senator or Governor?" Brinks needed to know.

"Or both, keep in mind that not everyone wants to see the City of Kinloch rebuilt." added Banker Bob.

"Why do you think that is?" asks Brinks wanting to hear an objective opinion from a white man.

"I don't have to tell you how successful the City Of Kinloch was before so many people became addicted to drugs. Instead of trying to help their people get off, others saw an opportunity to get rich of their shortcomings, by supplying the product.

Then there were the elected City Officials who had the power to stop the epidemic; however, grew tired with the struggles and sold off or stole the cities assets and pocketed the money." said Banker Bob adding nothing that Brinks didn't already know,

"How did you come to that conclusion?" Brinks inquired knowing that Banker Bob knew more then what he was saying.

"Kinloch had plenty of money which is a universal language. I follow the money." was all that Banker Bob would say looking into Brinks eyes,

"I respect that, enough said. See what you can find out for me, I'll make it worth your while." said Brinks standing to leave.

"I'm on it." said Banker Bob putting up the sheet to cover the bars blocking anyone from looking into his cell, before pulling out his cell phone.

Walking up the eight flights of steps to get to his cell, Brinks ponders his conversation with Banker Bob, Everything he said held a ring of truth to it; too much truth.

Returning to his cell Brinks found Rain kneeling down stirring the food in their crock pots. Entering the cell he washes his hands while looking at Rain out of the corner on his eye, something is different about him he thought.

"How long are we going to keep tiptoeing around this conversation?" Brinks ask as he dries off his hands.

"I wanted to get my thoughts together before I told you. How did you know?" Rain asks, still sitting down on a chair.

"You move different, which isn't a bad thing." answered Brinks.

"Just got so much on my mind." Rain told him.

"I understand but you act like you got to deal with it alone." stated Brinks.

"Some things a man needs to handle on his own." stated Rain avoiding eye contact with Brinks

"I'm going to ignore that last comment. Dudes brothers won't be a problem so you can stop playing that situation over in your head." Brinks said instantly getting Rains full attention.

"What, how did you know?" asked Rain shocked.

"I would be considering the same things. Only a fool wouldn't." stated Brinks.

"What did you do?" asked Rain not sure how far Brinks had taken things.

"Wisdom came to see me today, I told him about the problem." answered Brinks.

"That's what I didn't want. They have some wonderful things going on and he needs to stay focused on that." said Rain not liking what brinks had done.

"You are family and you at a disadvantage Rain, you need help. Wisdom is very smart and won't put himself in a bad situation, relax." said Brinks.

"It must have been really important for him to come all the way up here? Asked Rain.

"They're having problems with city officials getting permits and approval for the projects." answered Brinks.

"Are they denying them for a good cause or extorting them?" ask Rain.

"What do you think." replied Brinks looking at Rain sideways.

"Something's never change, so how are we going to handle this?" Rain wanted to know.

"I got it." Brinks replied picking up Investors Business Daily and scanning the articles.

"So you're cutting me out?" asks Rain standing and now pacing the cell.

"Fallback, go home, I got this." replied Brinks while continuing to read the paper.

"Oh, so its like that?" asked Rain now standing in front of Brinks.

Setting the paper down Brinks looked up at Rain who obviously didn't like the way things were going.

"Have a seat, now you know how I feel." stated brings smiling at his cousin.

"You play too much." Rain said taking his seat.

Brinks explained to Rain everything that Wisdom had told him. Then he told him about his conversation with Banker Bob.

"Banker Bobs connections will come up with something." said Rain knowing that Banker Bob is all about his business.

"He will and when he does, we will put together a solid plan." stated Brinks as he began to formulate a strategy is his mind.

"Sounds good." Replied Rain now happy he had spoken with Brinks about things.

CHAPTER SEVEN

Leaving his house the next morning, Jamaal felt energized and ready to take on the world, If his first class was any indication of the things to come, he knew KOFUAA would be a great success. Arriving early he wanted to get his morning workout out of the way. In route to the gym he caught a glimpse of Pam and Janet sitting in the break room.

"Good morning." said Jamaal stepping into the break room making a beeline grabbing one of the protein bars from the cabinet.

"Good morning how was your first class?" asks Janet.

"It went really good, I had a lot of class participation." answered Jamaal

"That's good to hear, I was concerned that we wouldn't be perceived well." stated Pam.

"There will be challenges at times getting them to understand certain things but with patience we'll get through to them." Jamaal assured them.

"That's understandable, well we better get going, our class starts in 5 minutes." said Janet standing grabbing her things.

"I wish you well." said Jamaal finishing up his snack.

"Thanks." Pam replied as she followed Janet out of the break room.

Both women were feeling a bit more confident after their conversation with Jamaal and it showed in their walk. Entering the classroom dressed in business suits, it was clear that they meant business.

After setting their things down, Pam and Janet leaned back on the teacher's desk looking over the class before speaking.

"Good morning, I'm Pam and this Janet we will co-teach this class; Forward Thinking. Let's go around the room and make introductions before we begin." said Pam as Janet pointed from student to student who in turn stood and gave their name.

"Forward Thinking, is designed to teach you to focus on the big picture ahead while delaying instant gratification. This will result in financial freedom, an accumulation of assets, and less stress." said Janet

"I could use some of that." stated Shawn with the entire class agreeing.

"Everyone has a general idea of what money is but most people don't really understand how it really works, that's why it eludes the vast majority of people. Money is a tool no different from a hammer or an ax. Not knowing how to properly use either can and will hurt you. Do any of you play chess?" asks Janet causing some of the students to raise their hand.

"For those of you who don't, chess is a game of strategy. Part of that strategy is to send your soldiers out to capture other soldiers and bring them back. The rich see chess as more then just a game and have become great chess players who have mastered the art of strategy. While you send your soldiers (money) out to get murdered (spent), their soldiers go out and brings them back more money, your money." stated Janet looking around to make sure that she had their attention seeing a hand go up.

"Yes" said Janet.

"What if you don't have any soldiers to start with?"' asks Tina.

"All of us have soldiers to start with if you have ANY type of income coming in. Most experts recommend that you should save 10% of your income but each person's situation is different. We recommend that you save at least 20% of your after-tax income once you have gotten your debt under control. Even when you are trying to get it under control we want you to save something, even if it's only $20. If you're in a position to sock away even more, go ahead and save as much as possible. I encourage you to save until it hurts, NO pain, no gain." said Janet.

"How do you get ahead with saving so little?" asks Jackie.

"Starting small will turn saving into a habit and this in turn with cause what you have to grow." answered Janet.

"We want you to get out of debt while contributing to your retirement plan. This is easier accomplished then most people realize. Most of you are young and can take on a side job or business allowing that full income to pay off your debt while avoiding decades of interest. Making contribution to your retirement is key and you could continue this side job or business for a little while until you've saved a few dollars." said Pam.

"That sounds like all work and no play." said Shawn

"It can be but you dug the hole, be man enough to dig you way out." stated Pam challenging him.

"I'm man enough to do it!" stated Shawn

"Good because I'll be on your ass making sure that you do." stated Pam looking at him.

"We don't want you to just put the money into an account that pays 0.01 percent interest. There are ways to earn a safe higher return on your nest egg. Such as online high-yield savings accounts and other institutions offer interest rates far above the national average. Moving this savings online will keep that money separate from your checking account, therefore making it harder to use for impulse buys. You should also look into reward checking accounts from small, local banks or credit unions. These accounts usually offer higher rates than online savings accounts if you meet certain requirements, such as making a minimum number of debit-card purchases each month and agreeing to receive statements electronically." Janet educated them.

"I could do that." Jackie replies feeling a bit more optimistic about her future.

"All of you can with some discipline. Building a safeguard of savings in the bank is like buying business insurance, a solid cash cushion that will allow you to survive whatever the economy throws your way." said Pam looking out over the class.

"Are there any questions?' asks Janet

"Yea, when can we get started?" ask Shawn.

"Today" answered Pam reaching into her pocket pulling out a stack of debt cards. "Each one of you will receive $100 to start your account with, but don't get this twisted, this ain't all gravy, and were not into tricking. You will give us permission to monitor your account until it is determined that you are on the right track. Does anyone have en objection to that?" Janet asks looking around.

"You don't trust us?" ask Shawn.

"HELL NO, you've established a pattern of making bad decisions. We want to help you change that by showing you how to make good decisions which builds trust." said Pam looking directly at Shawn.

"Damn, that was direct but I like it that way. I'll work on it," said Shawn

Pam removed her laptop setting it onto the desk. The entire class gathered around listening and observing as she demonstrated how to research bank and credit unions for the best rates. Then she showed them how to open up a high interest account for the $100 that they would receive.

"Each of you will receive a booklet that will walk you through the process step-by-step that I just showed you. I expect you to study it and check the different institution regularly for changes in rates. If you find something that's better with a higher rate, move your money, and share it with others. Are there any question'" ask Pam.

No one raised their hand.

"Well then our time is up for today, Janet will hand everyone a debt card that has the $100 dollars on it. Grab a booklet and head down to the computer lab and get started. When you are done, please bring us your password. Have a blessed day." said Pam as Janet moved about the room handing out debt cards.

"Next time class we will discuss the 529 education savings accounts that will pay for college for your kids. Assets in these accounts enjoy tax-free growth, and withdrawals from them are tax-free when used for tuition and other qualified expenses." Janet told than before dismissing them.

As the students filed out of the class room they were greeted by Man-Man and Big Hands coming to check on Janet and Pam.

"How was class?" asks Man-Man.

"It went great." they answer in unison laughing.

"That's good, glad I didn't have to straighten nobody out about you." said Big Hands hugging Pam.

"Hey, get a room." said Janet playfully.

"Why this desk will do," said Pam bending over the desk assuming the position with a devilish smile.

"That's what I'm talking about." said Big Hands smacking her on the ass.

"You two are out of control," said Janet grabbing Man-Man's hand trying to pull him out of the classroom.

"Hold up babe, let's watch." said Man-Man smiling
"Boy, come on, I got something for you to watch."
said Janet winking at him.
"That's all you had to say!" Said Man-Man
rubbing his hands together and following Janet out of
the room.

CHAPTER EIGHT

Richard Payne had accomplished something that most young men from Kinloch had not, avoided the game. It wasn't that he didn't have the opportunity, he did; his brother is a major player.

The money, street fame, and women meant nothing to him. Richard even refused to accept gifts from his brother. Most of the younger guys thought that he was crazy opting instead to work for the maintenance department of the Boaz Projects.

While most of the guys he knew went to prison, became strung out on drugs, or got murdered. Richard went on to climb the corporate ladder becoming Vice President of a Fortune 500 Company before he quit and started his own private equity firm. Although he wasn't Tiger Woods rich, Richard could afford to live life on his own terms.

Married with three kids, Richard attends church services every Sunday at the church across the street from the Boaz Projects that he has attended since a kid.

"Richard Payne" said Wisdom extending his hand greeting Richard as he and his family exited the church.

"Wisdom Jones, I haven't seen you in years. This is my wife Betty and our children Richard Jr., Raymond, and Rachel." said Richard making the introductions.

"Nice to meet all of you." said Wisdom shaking each of their hands.

"I didn't see you inside." said Richard trying to feel Wisdom out.

"I wasn't but don't give up on me. I was hoping that I could speak with you a moment." said Wisdom.

"Sure, Betty, I'll be with you all in a moment." said Richard handing his wife the keys to the truck.

"Is everything alright?' ask Betty concerned having heard of Wisdom's reputation.

"Yes, Wisdom and I go way back but under different circumstances." said Richard comforting his wife.

Walking through the church parking lot, Wisdom and Richard strolled into Kinloch Park grabbing a seat on one of the benches.

"So what's on your mind Wisdom?" Richard asks

"Have you heard about the Kinloch Organization for Uplifting African Americans?" Wisdom replies.

"Yes, some of the church members have been reporting great things about it." answered Richard.

"My past isn't one that I'm proud of, I can't change it, however; through KOFUAA I'm trying to make amends." Wisdom explained.

"Have you sought forgiveness from God?" ask Richard looking at Wisdom closely.

"I have. I'm saved and believe whole heartily that hehas forgiven me." stated Wisdom looking directly at Richard.

"I'm happy to hear that, what's on your mind?" Richard asks curiously.

"I want you to run for Mayor, hear me out."

said Wisdom stopping Richard before he could respond.

"Go on." said Richard not totally surprised by Wisdom's ambitions.

"The City of Kinloch needs someone like you who is incorruptible, who will lead, teach, and not hesitate to make unpopular decisions that will benefit the people as a whole." said Wisdom.

"I'm honored that you consider me the best person for the job. Honestly this is something that I've always wanted to do but money alone won't win an election. I need to know more about what's going on. And I couldn't give you an answer before speaking with my wife about this first." said Richard looking at Wisdom.

"I respect that. I'm not asking you to be the Mayor in name only. You will have complete control, no strings attached." Wisdom assures him.

"That's good to know. A lot of changes must be made and jobs created. I would want to start with a new Chief of Police, do you have anyone in mind?" Richard asks.

"I do, Nathan Boxer." replied Wisdom smiling at Richard.

"I was thinking the same thing." said Richard liking the plan more and more.

"You will need a staff that you can trust, also KOFUAA will soon begin the first of three phases rebuilding and jobs are on the way." Wisdom assured him.

"The election is in a couple of months. I'm not sure that's enough time to prepare, Mayor Brown is no pushover." stated Richard.

"Let me worry about those types of things, I just need to know if you are on board?" asked Wisdom looking at Richard letting him know that he is dead serious about this.

"We need to have an understanding about a couple of things. One I'm not participating in ANYTHING illegal to get into office, and two if I win I will come after you or anyone else who breaks the law." said Richard making sure there was no misunderstandings,

"I wouldn't have it any other way, that's why I want you. Now please go speak with your wife, time is of the essence." said Wisdom.

"Okay, give me a minute." said Richard as he made his way back over to his truck as his wife was stepping out of it.

After several intense moments, Richard returned with Betty blazing a trail towards Wisdom.

"Wisdom you probably don't remember me because I wasn't one of those loose girls. I love this City just a much as both of you but I love my family more. I remember how you use to do things but I'm not scared of you. If you want my approval, I need to hear you say that my husband will be able to do his job without you trying to influence him in any way." said Betty watching Wisdom closely.

"You have my word." said Wisdom admiring Betty.

"Then we have an election to win." said Betty as Richard and Wisdom smiled at one another.

"I've hired some political consultants, you will announce that you are running immediately." said Wisdom

"I can handle the financing, we just need to figure out how to win." said Richard knowing that it wouldn't be easy.

"We will find a way." said Wisdom shaking both of their hands before walking off.

"Can we trust him" asked Betty.

"Yes." replied Richard who was a lot more familiar with Wisdom than Betty would ever know.

CHAPTER NINE

Jamaal causally strolled up the sidewalk admiring all of the people and fine automobiles that crowded both sides of Kinloch Park. There were so many people from all over St. Louis present to celebrate Kinloch Day with the first all African American City in Missouri.

The news media was out and about conducting interviews with St. Louis finest. Nelly and Murphy Lee were being interviewed about up coming projects; Chingy is judging the talent show with Cedric The Entertainer, Huey is posted up watching as Kimora Lee Simmons scouts new talent for an up coming project. People were moving around enjoying themselves eating from different vendors, participating in tournaments which included horseshoes, softball, and volleyball just to name a few.

Others were enjoying the talent show awaiting the performances that would come later by the all star line up courtesy of some or Kinloch's finest incarcerated in federal facilities who reached out to their celebrity friends to show their support. Rumors were spreading that Young Jeezy would be performing with T.I.

Some of the guys that Jamaal grew up with that were still hustling sat under the big tree on the steps as he was strolling by and decided to stop briefly to greet them.

"Glad to see so many people at Kinloch Day." said Jamaal.

"Why don't you come around anymore?" asked Craig ignoring Jamaal's comment.

"We parted ways on good terms, I have nothing but love for you all." said Jamaal looking at them.

"I can't tell you don't come around anymore." said Ace.

"That's because our ships don't sail in the same direction. I'm not knocking you, I've been there but I'm not there anymore. You see I don't like being in a cage and I'm not going to rat on anyone so I stay away." said Jamaal.

"You think hanging around us is going to get you a case?" asked Ace.

"It's been known to happen and probably will if I allow it, Conspiracy is a catch all law that I don't want to get caught up in. Even if I don't get convicted, I'll spend good hard earned money paying a lawyer to defend me." Jamaal explained as he began to walk off.

"Prison has really changed you and made you scary." said Craig looking disgusted with Jamaal.

"You see love is the most powerful weapon in the world, stronger than hate, fear, and even death. Back then I didn't give a fuck and didn't mind murking something if need be. Scared, I'll never be that, I'm not that smart. Prison, ha-ha, how can I fear something that I've experienced? I got love for my people now; this should give a lot of people comfort." Jamaal said looking each one of them in the eye.

"Yea, whatever" said Craig taking a pull from the Kush.

"I've survived the worst that could be done to me. You continue to play the game. So we'll see how well you do when it's your turn up to bat." said Jamaal smiling and walking off knowing that everyone in the game would unquestionably get a chance to bat.

"Walking through the crowds Jamaal was greeted by several of the students that attend his class. In the distance, he spots Deputy Mayor Washington and excuses himself. Making a beeline straight for him Jamaal stops and then waits until he is about to walk away then approaches.

"Deputy Mayor." said Jamaal getting his attention.

"Jamaal, it's nice to see you out and about." said the Deputy Mayor smiling feeling that Jamaal is a bird nest on the ground.

"Same here, you good?" asked Jamaal making sure that he received the money.

"Yes, you are a man of your word, I like that, step over here. Mayor Brown has been made aware of your generous donation and funding the purchase of the tickets to the "Kinloch Day" event; he appreciates the way you do business. We will need another $10,000 for the benefit of Browns Campaign prior to the election and another $10,000 after the election." The Deputy informed him.

"No problem, just make sure the Mayor helps us out, expediting our projects." said Jamaal trying not to show his contempt.

"Absolutely." replied the Deputy Mayor thinking that the conversation went easier than he expected it to.

"Give me ten minutes and I'll grab the checks for you." stated Jamaal.

"I'll wait here." replied the Deputy Mayor.

Jamaal secured checks from straw donors for the $10,000 contribution and then delivered them to the Deputy Mayor. After confirming the checks did not exceed the contribution limit the Deputy Mayor accepted them placing them in his pocket.

"Jamaal I can assure you that your project will be approved by the Mayor, I can't guarantee anything else. Have you meet with Tyron Price? The Deputy Mayor asked him.

"You already know the answer to that question." stated Jamaal not liking the way the Deputy Mayor was trying to carry him.

"I do, you shouldn't put it off any longer." suggested the Deputy Mayor smiling at Jamaal.

"I'll take care of it, please step a little closer so no one can hear us." requested Jamaal before leaning in close to the Deputy Mayor.

The Deputy Mayor complied; in a low menacing voice speaking in a whisper so that only the Deputy Mayor could hear, Jamaal told him.

"The will find you two cocksuckers in pieces if you cross us." Jamaal uttered causing the blood to drain from the Deputy Mayor's face.

"Jamaal there is no need for threats." the Deputy Mayor said nervously trying to compose himself.

That's not a threat, it's a reality. We paid you greedy motherfuckers, you better come through." stated Jamaal looking deep into the Deputy Mayor's eyes before walking off leaving him shaken.

"Jason, Jason." repeated Mayor Brown trying to get the Deputy Mayors attention.

"Yes, sorry sir, what do you need?" asks the Deputy Mayor still trying to pull himself together.

"What's wrong with you, you look like you just saw a ghost? asked Mayor Brown.

"If they don't get approved, we will be ghost." the Deputy Mayor stated looking into the Mayors eyes.

"What? you are over reacting; we are going to milk those thugs for as much as we can, then dismiss them." replied the Mayor brushing off the comment.

The Deputy Mayor grabbed the Mayor by the arm pulling him to the side before speaking.

"Listen, your arrogance is going to get us both murdered. I told you from the beginning that these people weren't the type that you fuck over but your greedy ass blew me off. We're not going to force their hand, they paid us, and you will approve them. Do you understand me? asked the Deputy Mayor holding onto the Mayor's arm tightly looking into his eyes for confirmation.

"Okay, Okay, now let me go." replied the Mayor snatching his arm away smoothing out his suit.

****

In the meantime, Wisdom was trying to handle the situation with Rain. Uncle Ronnie was the only person whom he had spoken to about Rain's situation being that everyone else would no doubt overreact.

Uncle Ronnie had been conducting surveillance on the brothers for over a month learning their routine.

By all appearances these two weren't the brightest but they were intent on extracting revenge for their brother's death Uncle Ronnie quickly observed.

Following them was easy and so was determining when they would try to strike, clearly these guys weren't thinking straight. What they didn't know was that Rain would not be where they predicted.

Driving a late model Suburban with tinted windows, Uncle Ronnie turned onto 1st St, instantly spotting the two in a dark Chevy circling the block of St. Louis Community Release Center; the halfway house.

Pulling out in front of them, Uncle Ronnie drove at a slow pace until he reached a stop sign. Swooping up behind them, Wisdom used the Dodge Ram he was driving to block then in before hopping out of the truck suited and booted.

Kicking open the back door of the Suburban, Uncle Ronnie with a Ski Mask on held a AK-47 aimed at the two catching them off guard, giving Wisdom the opportunity to slide into the backseat wearing gloves and a ski mask aiming the 44 Magnum at the driver.

"Gentlemen, don't try to be a hero, be smart and place your hands on your head." Wisdom firmly ordered.

"Who the fuck are you? asked the one in the passenger seat while complying.

"A nightmare you don't need and the last person you will see if you don't do as I say! Therefore, it is in your best interest that we reach an understanding!" Wisdom told them.

"Look man, we don't know what you want, we ain't got no money." said the driver pleading with Wisdom.

"Did you tell your kids that you love them before you left home?" Wisdom asks.

"What?" said the shocked driver.

"When you left home you should have told your children that you love them being that there is no assurances that you will make it back."

"I don't know who the fuck you are but we don't have any beef with you!" said the passenger.

"Both of you have wives and kids that love you. Your emotions have prevented you from looking at the past and the future before making the decision to kill Rain." said Wisdom now having their attention.

"He murdered our brother" spat the passenger.

"He did but was your brother not in the wrong? He was a jackboy and he knew the consequences for his actions." stated Wisdom hoping that he could reason with the two.

Neither said anything. Wisdom went on.

"Had someone done to you what your bother did to rain, you would have reacted the same way. It's not always easy to put your emotions to the side and say that someone you love fucked up but it's the responsible thing to do." Wisdom said silently praying that he was getting through to them.

"So you want us to let this ride? The driver said angrily.

"I'm asking you to look into the future. Consider your kids growing up without fathers or with a stepfather who is abusive, while their mother struggles because you are dead." stated Wisdom letting the words sink in.

The men sat thinking not saying a word.

"I'm going to relieve you of your weapons and allow you to go on with your life. As you can see you have been under surveillance and will continue to be. Move on with your lives or loose them" said Wisdom before exiting the car.

CHAPTER TEN

Rain decided to take the Grey Hound home so that he could have some time to think while enjoying the scenic route. 20 years had passed since had been free and so much had changed. The outside world seemed so different although some things were the same.

Stopping in Kingdom City to switch buses Rain was surprised to see Wisdom waiting on him as the bus pulls in. Stepping off the bus, he couldn't do anything but smile at his younger cousin.

"How did you know?" asked Rain smiling

"I would have done the same thing." Replied Wisdom

"I needed to get my thoughts together." Rain explained.

"I understand that's why I gave you some time to do so. I watched you get on the bus in Jefferson City." Wisdom admitted.

"Remind me to stay on your good side." said Rain joking but was dead serious.

"Let's get going." said Wisdom getting into the truck.

"This is nice." said Rain referring to the custom Moonshine White Cadillac Wisdom was driving.

"You don't have to worry about dude's brothers, we have an understanding." Wisdom informed Rain once they were in the truck.

"What type of understanding?" ask Rain looking at Wisdom.

"Let's just say they understand that they have a bright future if they let things go." Wisdom replied.

"Can we trust them?" ask Rain

"Trust, never but they have more to loose then gain and now they realize it!" Wisdom answered.

"If you say it's cool, then that's what it is." said Rain appreciating everything.

"Glad you like the truck, its yours." stated Wisdom looking over at Rain.

"Get the fuck out of here." was all that Rain could say.

"Real talk." Wisdom told him.

"Thanks, but there's a problem." Rain said looking over at Wisdom.

"What?" Wisdom asked confused.

"I don't like anyone driving my shit!. run those keys youngster." said Rain extending his hand.

Smiling Wisdom handed Rain the keys, got out and walked around to the passenger side getting in. Rain slid over into the driver's seat, adjusting the seat and mirror.

"Where are my CD's? asks Rain looking around.

"All of your music is on the IPOD, just stroll down until you find the album you want, and then select the song." Wisdom instructed.

Rain scrolled through the list of albums before stopping at the Isaac Brother's, finding the song he was looking for, Rain turns up the volume as "Drifting on a Memory" begins to boom out of the speakers.

Putting the truck in drive, Rain nodded at

Wisdom before pulling off. The drive back to St. Louis is smooth with each man off in his own thoughts.

Wisdom gave Rain directions to his home were Rain dropped him off before heading to his house. Pulling into his driveway things looked the same just better, he thought. Hopping out of his truck Rain rushed to the door and then began knocking really hard

"Who the fuck is that knocking on my door like that?" Jane was saying as she opened the door only to find Rain standing there.

"The last time I check this was our house." He said as she ran into his arms hugging him real tight.

"When did you get out? Why didn't you call me to come pick you up? And who'd truck is that?" she asked excitedly.

"Calm down, I got out today, wanted to surprise you, and the truck is a gift from Wisdom." He told her.

"You did a good job of surprising me, now get in here. You should have told me I would have gotten my hair and my nails done." said Jane.

"Woman you stay looking beautiful besides, I'm going to sweat your hair out anyway!" said Rain, pulling his wife in close to him Rain's hands roamed her body as he kissed her passionately.

"That feels goooooood" she moaned leaning into him.

"Unable to stand it any longer, Rain wrestled Jane's jeans off and sits her on the edge of the loveseat facing him. Spreading her legs wide, Jane invites Rain to tear her little pussy up but that would have to wait.

Kneeling Rain pressed his face into her pussy, his tongue penetrating her causing her to make incoherent sounds. Her knees buckle a little as he dips his tongue in and out of her wetness. She continues to make slow moaning sounds as he thoroughly devours her sweet, succulent pussy while Jane rides his face.

"Ahhhhhhh Rain, damn baby I missed you so much." Jane cried out as a flood of wetness gushed from her onto his tongue and lips.

"Enter me." she demands as Rain gets to his feet.

After removing his clothes, Rain enters Jane as she wraps her legs around his back and arms around his neck. With long deep strokes, he begins to make love to his wife.

"Get this pussy daddy, make me cum." she croons missing him being inside her.

Feeling the same way, Rain dug in and out of his wife until his knees began to tremble as they both climaxed.

"I love you, don't ever leave me again." Said Jane holding his face and looking into his eyes.

"I won't baby, I wont" he replies looking deep into her eyes before passionately kissing her.

Awaking early the next morning refreshed, Rain is ready to begin the new chapter of his life only to find Jane missing.

Putting on his robe, he heads down the steps where he sees his daughter Robin, and grandson Robbie sitting at the kitchen table having breakfast.

"Grandpa," yells Robbie jumping out of his chair and running over to his grandfather.

"How's my big man doing?" Rain asked his grandson picking him up.

"Fine" he replies giggling.

"Dad, why didn't you tell me you were coming home yesterday?" his daughter asks pouting stealing a piece of his heart.

"Come give me a hug before you start interrogating me." requested rain which she did.

"Dad are you ignoring me?" she asked not letting him off the hook.

"I wanted to surprise everyone." He replied.

"You knew I wanted to pick you up but I'll forgive you this time." She said.

"Thank you." said Rain playing with his grandson.

"What do you have planned for the day?" Asked Robin.

"Robbie and I are going over to KOFUAA while you two go get dolled up." Said Rain.

"That sounds good to me." said Jane liking the idea.

"Me too." Added Robin.

"I'm going with grandpa!" yelled an excited Robbie.

After showering and getting dressed, Rain and Robbie headed over to KOFUAA. He heard about all the changes made to the city of Kinloch; however he wasn't prepared for what he saw. Where houses, businesses, churches and apartments once stood, the land was flat, cleared of everything, this he simply couldn't understand.

How is it that the neighborhood he lived in, Ladue, hadn't changed, except for the better while Kinloch was totally destroyed, the building of that airport really fucked them around he thought to himself pulling into the parking lot.

Exiting the truck with Robbie in tow, Rain enters the building and is immediately impressed with what has been done with the old Kinloch High School. Standing there brought back a lot of old memories of him attending the High School and the wild parties that were thrown there after it closed.

"Are you looking for someone?" asks Jihad with Jamaal Jr. by his side bringing Rain back to the present.

"Yes, is Jamaal around?" ask Rain

"Who should I say would like to see him?" asks Jamaal Jr.

"Rain" he replied

"Oh, follow us." said Jamaal Jr. recognizing the name.

Upon entering the library Rain is surprised to see Jamaal, Wisdom, Uncle Ronnie and two other gentlemen that he didn't know with books spread across the tables.

"I'll be damn, Rain get over here!" ordered Uncle Ronnie standing to embrace his sister's son.

"Hey, Uncle Ronnie, you looking good." said Rain as they embraced.

"Thanks, have you been to see your mother?" ask Uncle Ronnie.

"No, it's too early, that's my next stop." Rain assured him.

"You're a sight for sore eyes, we could use some more help." said Jamaal standing to embrace Rain.

"Let me know where I fit in." replied Rain.

"Robbie can hang out with Jihad and Jamaal Jr., Justice will be here in a minute." said Wisdom

"Come on Robbie." said Jihad grabbing Robbie's hand as they ran out of the library.

"This is Hakim and Dank" said Uncle Ronnie making the introductions.

"I've heard a lot of good things about both of you." said Rain shaking both of their hands.

"Likewise." said Dank with Hakim agreeing

Grabbing a seat, Rain sat listening as they brought him up to speed on all of the things that they had going on, he is impressed.

"We were thinking that you could run Teach One with Dank, it's an incubator for small business." said Uncle Ronnie

"Sounds good to me." replied Rain now feeling like apart of the team.

****

Later that same day Jamaal had his first meeting with Tyrone Price to discuss the process for obtaining relief from existing zoning regulations and the cost for Peter Johnson's approval. The meeting is being held at Frank's Place at the bottom of Kinloch, a place were neither would stick out.

"Good afternoon." said Tyrone strolling through the door were he found Jamaal sitting in a both waiting on his food.

"Thanks for agreeing to meet me, I ordered cheese burgers, chicken wings, and fries." Jamaal informs Tyrone as he slid into the opposite side of the booth.

"Sounds good, this is a very ambitious project you're taking on." said Tyrone getting straight down to business.

"It is but nothing we can't handle. The question is can you handle your end?" Jamaal asks looking directly at him.

"Certainly, as long as you handle yours." replied Tyrone confidently.

"Jamaal your order is ready" sang Sam a pretty female working the counter.

"Thanks Sam." Jamaal flirts getting up to grab their order before heading back over to the booth setting the tray down before sliding in.

"Mr. Johnson will handle the zoning official and the Mayor." said Tyrone taking a bite out of his sandwich.

"How much?" ask Jamaal applying hot sauce to his wings.

"$30,000 for me and $100,000 for him." replied Tyrone testing the waters.

"You all are a bit greedy, wouldn't you say?" asked Jamaal wanting to reach across the table and strangle his ass.

"This process is complicated and we've did our homework, your crew has plenty." replied Tyrone looking at Jamaal.

"If you did your homework then both of you should understand that no one gets a pass." Stated Jamaal making sure that Tyrone understood him.

"Ha-ha calm down, we can definitely help you get through a lot of the red tape." replied Tyrone is feeling a bit uncomfortable with Jamaal's subtle threat but believing it.

"Give me a minute" said Jamaal getting up step outside of Frank's Place,

After several minutes of speaking with Dank and Hakim, he walks back into the restaurant.

"The money is in the backseat of your car, every dime you asked for. Now it would be in both of your best interests not to take this money if you have no intentions of doing what you said you would do." Jamaal warns him still standing looking into Tyrone's eyes.

"We will but we don't accept cash" Tyrone was saying before Jamaal cut him off.

"You do now! launder it yourself." Jamaal said before walking off leaving Tyrone dumbfounded.

CHAPTER ELEVEN

Richard Payne made it official that he was throwing his hat into the race for Mayor. Mayor Brown in response laughed and made mockery not considering Richard a real contender.

Now all Uncle Ronnie and Wisdom needed to do is come up with a way to keep Mayor Brown from winning a reelection. With no experience in politics both knew they needed someone who did and Uncle Ronnie knew just who. The problem is he is an ex-politician, a crook in Uncle Ronnie's eyes.

John Bacon was an unsuccessful Kinloch Mayoral Candidate in the election held on May 12, 2006 who got himself into some trouble, John along with Cliff his brother, who acted as his campaign manager and political advisor for the 2006 Mayoral election, made some really bad decisions.

Two individuals who previously accepted corrupt payments posed as informants and suggested that the informant meet with John to protect his real estate development interests in Kinloch. Over the course of six meetings, the informant agreed to make cash payments and illicit contributions to John's campaign in exchange for his future official assistance, action and influence. The Bacon's accepted three cash payments from the informant totaling $37,500 prior to the election. The informant also agreed to pay the Bacon's an additional $22,500 after John was elected, in exchange for John's official assistance as mayor.

Mike Glover served as a Commissioner on the Kinloch Housing Authority and was also the affirmative action officer for St. Louis County. Paul Kelly was an employee of the Kinloch Department of Health and Human Services. A separate scheme was hatched involving these two.

First, John agreed to expedite approvals of a Kinloch real estate development project known as the "Monroe Development." In exchange, the informant paid the Bacon's $20,000 before the election and promised to pay an additional $10,000 after John was elected. Second, John agreed to promote Glover and Kelly in exchange for a payment of $11,500 before the election and the promise of an additional $11,500 after the election.

The election was held on May 12, 2006, and John received 36% of the vote, finishing second in a three-candidate field. Mayor Oscar Brown received 57% of the vote and was re-elected. Because John was not elected mayor, he did not receive either of the two post-election payments that were agreed upon in furtherance of the two schemes. However all of these transaction were recorded, John was arrested and subsequently pled guilty for accepting bribes receiving 60 months in Federal Prison.

"I don't like dealing with these slimy politicians." said Wisdom.

"Me neither but who better to show us how to beat Mayor Brown?" questioned Uncle Ronnie.

"I know, so where can we find him?" asked Wisdom.

"He owns the junk yard at the bottom of Kinloch, next door to United Construction but, I hear he spends his time fishing while someone covers for him." Replied Uncle Ronnie.

"What, are you sure, I thought Sam owned that?" asks Wisdom.

"Sam is his half-brother. John never liked getting his hands dirty but he must have a job being on federal parole." said Uncle Ronnie

"Let's pay him a visit." said Wisdom standing.

"We should find him at or rear the Alton Dam fishing." said Uncle Ronnie getting to his feet.

On the drive, Wisdom couldn't help but think about how corrupt this entire process was. Here it is they are trying to do something positive yet were constantly being prevented from doing so. He'd never thought that he would face so much opposition by those whom were elected to better the community.

From the highway Uncle Ronnie spotted John's truck. Wisdom turned off the exit taking the gravel road down to the river. Exiting the truck they were greeted by two Pit Bulls.

"Call off your dogs." yelled Uncle Ronnie removing the 44 Magnum from his waist.

"Parela" John yelled in Spanish, causing the dogs to go back to playing.

"Must be nice." said Uncle Ronnie admiring John's setup.

"It is. I knew you would be to see me. I like what you are doing, how may I assist you?" asked John offering them a seat.

"How did you know" Uncle Ronnie is curious to know.

"Because you know that I would have beaten Brown if it wasn't for my mishaps." stated John.

"I had you winning." Uncle Ronnie admitted.

"We all make mistakes. I think what you all are doing is great. How can I help you achieve your goal?" asked John not wanting to be remained on the past.

"We have someone that we think can beat Brown however, our knowledge of politics is very limited, that's were you come in." said Uncle Ronnie

"Who do you have to run against him?" John asks.

"Richard Payne." replied Wisdom.

"I don't know him, who is he?" asked John

"He grew up down in the Boaz Apartments. His people were moving major work but he wouldn't participate in any way. When we were out hustling he was working for the Boaz Apartments, he has a lot of love for the hood." stated Wisdom.

"But does he know anything about

politics?" asked John looking at Wisdom.

"No, but he's a very smart and successful businessman. With your help, we will guide him to victory." answered Wisdom,

"Like a straw man or puppet?" asked John looking closely at them.

"No. We will help him until he gets an understanding of things, then he's independent; free to do what's best for the City Of Kinloch." stated Uncle Ronnie.

"In exchange for what?" asked John.

"Nothing, we don't seek to control the neighborhood or its assets." Stated Uncle Ronnie.

"Just to be its protectors? John asked.

"You can say that, if we don't look out for our people then who will?" asked Wisdom.

"I see your point. You must get rid of the Chief of police too. Do you have anyone in mind?" John inquires.

"Nathan Boxer, he too grew up in the Boaz and refused to participate in the game. He now works for the St. Louis County Police." stated Wisdom.

"So it is your belief that these two can't be corrupted?" asked John.

"It is." answered Wisdom.

"John, what's your price to aid and assist us?" asked Uncle Ronnie getting straight to the point.

"I know that you think I am a piece of shit because of what went down. I'll admit, I was greedy like so many others; however, I always wanted what was best for the neighborhood." said John.

"Your price." asked Wisdom paying his speech no attention.

"In prison I made a decision, if I wasn't going to help, then I wouldn't hurt the situation. I would like to see the neighborhood rebuilt and restored. I'll help you free of charge, no strings attached." stated John with a sincere look in his eye.

"John you know you won't get a pass either?" asked Uncle Ronnie.

"What do you mean?" asked John.

"I mean that chop shop you running wont be protected." said Wisdom.

"What chop-shop?" John asked innocently

Uncle Ronnie produced the photos that had been taken of the cars moving in and out of his junkyard.

"Ha- Ha, I respect that." said John admiring the two.

"So how do we win the election? Asked Wisdom

John sat back pondering the entire situation before stating "There won't be an election."

"What are you talking about?" asked Uncle Ronnie

"Brown is in bed with Big Black, I have evidence to prove it. It's yours but the chop-shop stays." said John looking at them for their reaction.

"No deal, no one gets a pass. We'll find another way to win without you." said Uncle Ronnie standing to leave.

"Ronnie, Ronnie, please sit, I had to test you." said John getting Uncle Ronnie to take his seat.

"We don't just want them out of politics, we want

them gone for good." said Uncle Ronnie.

"Whoa, you know I don't get off into things like that." said John making his position clear.

"Not that type of gone, we want to make sure that they don't have anymore political ambitions." stated Wisdom.

"With the evidence that I have, you won't have a problem convincing them to leave town." John assured them before running over to his fishing pole that had a fish on the line.

****

CHAPTER TWELVE

KOFUAA has been taking up most of Jamaal's time leaving him mentally drained however that never stopped him from making all of his son's games. Today is no different, Jamaal, along with is mother, grandmother, and his oldest son sat in the stands cheering for his youngest son, Jihad who had scored a touchdown earlier.

"He reminds me so much of you when you played." said Ms. Burns.

"You were always scared that he would get hurt." said her mother Ms. Thomas

"That's my baby." replied Ms. Burns knowing that she couldn't win an argument with her mother.

"Girl that boy is tough as nails, hell I worried about him hurting someone else but never himself." laughed Ms. Thomas.

"Dad did you enjoy football?" asked Jamaal Jr

"I did." replied Jamaal.

"Why did you quit?" asks Jamaal Jr

"Bad decisions" replied Jamaal looking at his mother with apologetic eyes.

Out of the corner of his eye, Jamaal spotted Deputy Mayor Washing coming towards him. Excusing himself, Jamaal stood and hurried towards him, cutting him off before he could reach them.

"Jamaal, I heard that I could find you here, whose winning?" asks the Deputy Mayor

"I'm not giving you another dime." said Jamaal through clenched teeth.

"There's no need. I came to tell you that your project has been approved on all levels. You may begin construction immediately." said the Deputy Mayor hoping that the news would take the edge off Jamaal.

"That's great news, have a safe day." said Jamaal leaving the Deputy Mayor standing, pondering his last comment.

Before walking back over to take his seat, there was a call that Jamaal needed to make. Opening up his phone, he dialed a number and waited.

"RING, RING. RING"

"Hello"

"Sky, we've been approved." said Jamaal. overjoyed.

"What, when. that's great." said Sky

"A few minutes ago, I want to get started ASAP... said Jamaal.

"So do I. I'll call George our General Contractor as soon as I hang up." said Sky.

"Great, I'll stop by when I leave the game." said Jamaal before ending the call.

CHAPTER THIRTEEN

Before exiting the truck Wisdom said a silent prayer dreading the encounter, praying it would go smoothly. Although he wanted to go alone, Big Hands convinced him that doing so was a bad idea.

Wisdom stood watching the street packed with youngsters doing hand to hand out in the open, some things hadn't changed he thought.

"This is crazy." said Wisdom standing in front of his truck observing the transactions.

"This use to be us." said Big Hands.

"Hell naw, look around, there's no protection. Where are they going to run when the police come? How will they get rid of the money or product without being seen?" asked Wisdom not needing an answer.

"I see what you mean." said Big Hands looking around.

"Who yall looking for?" asked a youngster no older then 16.

"Those who have ears to hear." Stated Wisdom.

"What the fuck are you talking about?" asked the youngster as two more youngsters approached.

"Who are they?" asked the older one.

"I don't know but if they ain't buying, they need to keep it moving." replied the youngster.

"I'm Wisdom and this is Big Hands, We grew up around here and now run the Kinloch Organization for Uplifting African Americans." stated Wisdom as he scanned them for weapons.

"Congratulation but if you ain't spending money, yall need to bounce." said the older one.

"We come in peace." said Wisdom as he and Big Hands lifted their shirts showing that they weren't armed.

"Maybe you didn't hear me, Regulators!." yelled the older one which obvious was a signal because everyone on the set stopped what they were doing and rushed over.

"What's wrong?" asked Corey a guy around Wisdom's age whom they knew.

"They act like they can't hear." said the older one revealing the 45 tucked in his pants.

"Wisdom, Big Hands, it's been a minute since I've seen you two, what can I do for you?'" Corey asks with a smirk on his face.

"Order your crew to stand down." said Wisdom in a soft but firm voice.

"Things have changed around here Wisdom, I run things now." replied Corey standing his ground.

"Look at the older boy's shirt." said Wisdom as a red beam locked onto his shirt.

"Keep looking." said Big Hands as red beams began beaming in on several of Corey's crew.

"What type of shit is this?" said Corey looking around. Wisdom ignored Corey and smiles at him.

"Let's get an understanding with them." said Wisdom into the wireless microphone he was wearing. Dank fired a single shot from the sniper rifle that had a silencer end infrared beam on it sending a bullet through the top of the red St. Louis fitted worn by Corey.

"What the fuck!" said Corey removing his hat to make sure that his head was still attached.

"What, you thought I was crazy enough to come down here unarmed and out gunned? Everyone keep your hands where they can see them and no bodies will drop." Wisdom instructed.

"Do as he said" yelled Corey hoping that none of them were stupid enough to buck Wisdom.

"Corey, you still trying to live Dope Boy fantasies using these youngsters, don't know better" stated Wisdom looking into Corey's eyes.

"This is how we came up." said Corey in his own defense.

"It is and most of us went to prison, some died, while others ratted to stay free. You should be teaching them a better way being that you already know how things will end." said Big Hands.

"Then show us how to get this money the right way." said one of the youngsters.

"I'm not here to show you how to beat the game by exposing your flaws; there's no right way to do wrong. What you fail to understand is that there are too many unpredictable external factors working against you making the situation impossible to predict. Oprah Winfrey and Bob Johnson didn't start off flipping bricks, why do you think that you have too? Asked Wisdom.

"We trying to eat, why yall down here fucking with is?" Corey yells.

"Corey in all reality I couldn't care less about your rat ass but these youngsters who are following you deserve a chance." stated Wisdom.

"What is he talking about?" the youngster packing the 45 asks Corey.

"I'm talking about you all playing in a game that you can't win because it's not designed for you too. Corey ratted on some guys who are now doing football numbers in the feds. Most of the guys who know about it are either locked up or doing badly so they keep quiet because Corey has the work." said Wisdom letting the statement sink in.

"Is it true?" one of the youngsters asked Corey not receiving an answer.

"Yeah, it's true." said one of the youngsters obviously believing Wisdom and now despising Corey.

"There's so much you all don't know about this game, you're really at an unfair disadvantage. Even if you took Corey out of the equation, you still couldn't win. There are too many people you have to worry about and them telling on you; your customers, friends, family and even your connection. So what you don't touch their product, you think that makes your hands clean? Wrong, you're still going to prison." stated Wisdom.

"You come down here trying to knock us for trying to eat. I don't see you handing out hundred dollar bills." shot Corey.

"First off, check your tone. If you were trying to eat, there wouldn't be all these flashy cars parked out here nor would you waste money on all the jewelry you all are wearing. You don't have a goal to get some money and get out, you are hustling till the Feds come get you which is suicidal." said Big Hands receiving blank stares at the revelation.

"I'm trying to save your life. No one told us about prison or death being a part of the game. We jumped in head first not understanding the consequences being sucked in by the fruits of the poisonous tree. Some of you are standing there saying "fuck what he talking about"; however, this conversation will hit you like a ton of bricks when you're sitting in a federal holdover facing 20 to life" said Wisdom.

"We're not moving that type of work down here" Corey explained.

'It doesn't matter, you should know better. Your second State charge of Class A trafficking will get you a sentence that is without parole. I was locked up with guys who got caught with six grams of crack and got 25 years without parole in state prison." said Wisdom looking around hearing the sounds of disbelief.

"I look around and see that some of you have hate and murder in your eyes. You think that I'm trying to stop you from eating, I'm not. The life you are living is fast paced. Stop and think for a minute, how many people do you know that have beaten the game? How many of your brothers, father, and uncles have died or are in prison because of the game? There are so many brothers caged who made millions in these streets and don't have a dime. All they have are the memories of making it rain, blowing money fast, smoking dro, and the many females they slept with. They don't even have money to go to the canteen. Can you imagine coming home to nothing after all that money? This thing we call the game isn't designed for you to win. Yea, you may have stacked a few chips but the lawyers will enjoy what you've acquired. We've been damn fools for far too long, tricked into believing we can win ha-ha-ha, nothing is further from the truth. Look around, you all are no different then suicide bombers, the mission to get rich in these streets will end in a fatality, don't fool yourself." said Wisdom praying that he was getting through to them.

"So what do you expect us to do?" Corey asked Wisdom.

"I expect you to make a wise decision; this spot is officially shut down. You are all chasing a ghost that is elusive and your downfall is right around the corner. Any of you who would like a better way to live and get money without facing an early grave or prison, the doors of KOFUAA are open. I will personally show each of you how to make money legit while helping yourself and others, the choice is yours" said Wisdom looking out to all of them before walking back to his truck.

"Corey, you will be held responsible if this isn't shut down, you know how we rock." said Big Hands walking back to the truck hopping in.

"Do you think we got through to them?" ask Big Hands once inside the truck.

"To some yes." replied Wisdom.

"And Corey?" Big Hands asks.

"He will be the first one that we have to save." said Wisdom hopping back out of the truck to go and pull the youngster's off of Corey who was beating the shit out of him.

"That's enough" shouted Wisdom getting some of their attention while others continued to stomp Corey.

"BOOM, BOOM, BOOM" came Rain's 44 Magnum as he steps out of the bushes wearing Army fatigue followed by Dank, Man-Man, and Jamaal, bringing everything to a stand still.

"I know that you all feel betrayed by Corey but what you don't realize is that what he did was all a part of the game." said Wisdom

"So you saying that it's okay to rat on someone?' asks one of the youngster packing the 45.

"No I'm not, what I'm saying is that it's all a part of the game. You hear what they say these days. Tell on one and you get a time cut. Tell on three you to free. What type of shit is that? Most people try to choose what part of the game they are going to play, but it doesn't work like that. Kick doors, kidnapping, snitching, stealing, stunts, adultery, and murder are all a part of the game. Once you choose to be in the game then you are subject to all of those things that come along with it." Wisdom explained.

"But that shit right." replied a youngster

"There are no rules to the game, its illegal remember! You can't name one crew that was getting money and there wasn't a rat in the midst. Everyone enjoys the fruits of the hustle until its time to be judged by 12. When those indictments are hand down, dudes start doing the Nino Brown 'its bigger then me' or as you youngsters now call it "getting down first." This is even though you've chosen to be in the game." said Wisdom hoping that they were hearing him.

"This shit crazy" replied one the youngsters

"It is and that's what I'm trying to get you to understand." replied Wisdom praying that something that he was saying would sink in.

"Corey you should probably get moving before we leave or these youngsters well probably kill you." advised Dank helping him get to his feet.

"Obviously Corey isn't running anything anymore but that doesn't change what I said," stated Wisdom before walking back to his truck.

"Do you think that you got through to them?" ask Rain

"It's hard to say. Logic and reason doesn't govern anything out here." answered Wisdom.

"And if you didn't get through to them?' ask Rain.

"Next time we come through, we'll speak a

language they will understand." replied Jamaal.

****

At about the same time, Mayor Brown and the Deputy Mayor strolled into the barbershop greeting everyone before taking a seat to wait their turn. Uncle Ronnie and Hakim strolled in right behind them.

Approaching the Mayor, Uncle Ronnie takes the seat next to him, and then slips the newspaper containing a brown envelope inside into the Mayor's lap.

"What is this?" asks Mayor Brown looking at Uncle Ronnie like he is crazy.

"You might want to look at that in private. You two are finished in this town, gracefully bow out, and leave town." said Uncle Ronnie in a low voice that only the Mayor could hear.

Leaning over, the Mayor whispers something into the Deputy Mayor's ear which caused him to look at Uncle Ronnie. Standing, both men exit the barbershop followed by Uncle Ronnie and Hakim.

"What's inside the envelope?" the Deputy Mayor asks once they are outside.

"Pictures of you all doing business with Big Black, numbered accounts in the Caymans, safe deposit boxes located across the state, and a video of you requesting bribes from us." said Uncle Ronnie.

"I don't know who you think you are scaring." the Mayor was saying.

"WHOP. WHOP, WHOP," Hakim smacked the Mayor upside the head with a 357.

"Pay attention." said Hakim prepared to slap him again.

"I'm the Mayor" he said holding his head.

"WHOP", Hakim hit the Mayor again.

"Not anymore, I told you to pay attention."

"Okay, I hear you" said the Mayor holding his hands up in surrender.

"You two greedy bastards have eaten off the plate of this City for far too long, tomorrow you will withdraw from the race and both of you will disappear. Do I make myself clear?" ask Uncle Ronnie looking both them in the eyes.

"Yes" both men said in unison.

"Good, don't fuck with me.' said Uncle Ronnie before walking off followed by Hakim.

CHAPTER FOURTEEN

Wisdom discovers with great delight that he didn't simply love Justice just because she is his daughter but because of the friendship that they had formed. No matter what he had going on, he always found time each day to spend with her educating or picking her brain. This time of bonding is one that they both looked forward to each day.

"Why should you never accept being treated less than you're worth?" Wisdom asked his daughter.

"Because to do so would undermine my sense of self-worth which is fatal and because I am a Jones!" replied Justice with a smile.

"You better believe it." said Wisdom hugging his daughter.

"Dad, how did you stay strong all those years in prison?" Justice asked catching Wisdom off guard.

"I never told anyone this. When your Uncle Dammoe came to pick me up the day of the car show, before you were born, while riding I had a vision. The vision showed me that I would go to prison; and I would stay locked up a while and then get out. I brushed the vision off thinking nothing else of it. After leaving the car show everything started to unfold. When I got to the county jail this female guard came up to the bars one night and saw me studying my case. She told me to read Matthews: 10 every day and that God was going to do what he said he would do. I started to read Matthews everyday and continued to work on my case.

The day before my trail was to begin I came out of the visiting room and was walking past this preacher who stopped me. He said "God is going to do what he said he would do." This kind of freaked me out; I didn't say anything, I just walked off. The next day I started trial and things weren't looking good but I kept the faith. After several days of trail, the jury found me guilty. As I walked back to my cell a nurse stopped me and said "God is going to do what he said he would do." Irritated I just looked at her and walked off. The following day the jury recommended life with out parole. My faith wasn't shaken but I was depending more on myself then God to get me out of my situation. When I got to prison there was this guy they called Big Dog he was serving life without parole too. Big Dog was really into the bible. He approached me one day and said "God is going to do what he said he would do" and walked off. Now, I know that God can do anything but I thought that Big Dog was crazy along with everyone else. You see Big Dog would bring all of his things all the way from 7 walk down to the door saying that God said he was going home. He did this for almost the entire time I was there and then one day the Governor commuted his sentence from life without parole to life with and he was granted parole. I could have easily said that this guy just got lucky. Then I met this guy named Derrick, a crazy white guy. While sitting at the table doing some legal work I watched him walk past me with all his legal work, and then toss it on the trash. So I stopped him and told him that he should probably reconsider throwing away his legal work, especially being that he was on death row. He told me that God was going to save him and walked past me. A few months later the Pope came to St. Louis and asked the Governor to let Derrick off death row and he did. I was messed up because only god could have done something like that. I continued to work on my case, prayed and workout. The one day after my lawyer filed my Habeas Corpus I called your mother. She told me that she had a vision and God told her he was going to save me. Now I had never told her about my vision or these other incidents so this messed me up. After getting off the phone I went to the yard to walk the track clearing my thoughts, a voice or spirit said to me "If you look back on all the miracles that I've performed for you and others in the past, you will have no doubt that I will do what I said I would do." This made me realize that tripping off HOW God would do it caused me to waver in faith, from that day on I gave it to god. Less then a month later, God set me free." said Wisdom looking at his daughter.

"Wow, is that why you read the Bible and pray every morning?" Justice asked him.

"It is and so should you." replied Wisdom as Sky stepped into the room.

"What are you two talking about?" Sky asks looking at both of them with suspicious eyes before smiling.

"It's an inside thing mommy." replied Justice smiling at her father.

"Fine, keep your little secrets, go get ready we're taking your grandmother to the eye doctor." said Sky.

"Yes ma'am." said Justice.

"So, what will you do while were gone?" ask Sky

"Go work out." said Wisdom squeezing her ass.

'Watch it, you're going to get something started that we don't have time to finish." responded Sky.

"We got enough time." said Wisdom pinning her to the wall.

"I'm late." Said Sky

"Your mom can wait ten more minutes." said Wisdom planting kisses on her neck.

"No, the other late." said Sky causing him to stop.

"Are you pregnant?" Wisdom asked smiling

"I don't know yet, I will pick up a test while I'm out." She said smiling.

"That sounds good, get too it." said Wisdom releasing her and then smacking her on the ass as she walked off.

****

Meanwhile, George the General Contractor for United Construction had everything in place. He'd been waiting several months on Sky to give him the go ahead. Since receiving the call a couple of weeks ago, informing him that they had tall the necessary approvals, he's gotten a lot accomplished in such a short amount of time. KOFUAA would be built on the corner of Monroe, down the street from St. Michaels. Sky and Uncle Ronnie chose the location because it's easy access from highway 170 and Hanley road.

Uncle Ronnie and Jamaal arrived at the site not really expecting to see much happening. To their surprise George had the foundation laid and workers moving concrete forms. Getting out of the truck they were met by George.

"Good Morning, would either of you like a cup of coffee?" George offered.

"No thanks" both replied.

"If this is any indication of how fast this will be completed, we should be looking at five months?" Uncle Ronnie asked him.

"No, more like two. I'm bringing in two more contractors which will allow us to build faster. As you can see the foundation is complete. Most of the concrete forms are in place, we'll start filling them today." explained George.

"I like the idea of bringing in more workers, we need to get this done so we can move quickly to phase two." Said Uncle Ronnie

"I agree, phase two will take much longer." George told them.

"That's not a problem, we'll just have to work out of KOFUAA until its complete." said Jamaal.

"Is there anything that you need us to do?" asked Uncle Ronnie.

"No everything is under control." George assured them.

"Okay George, we'll let you get back to work." Said Uncle Ronnie before walking back to the truck followed by Jamaal.

"Is he dependable?" asked Jamaal.

"He's the one who did the work on Sky and Wisdoms house." Said Uncle Ronnie.

"That's reassuring." Said Jamaal.

CHAPTER FIFTEEN

Wisdom heads to his library to look over the documents that Rain had given him a second time before making a copy and placing the originals in his safe. Some things just never seemed to amaze him he though as he headed to his truck on his way to the gym.

Arriving, Wisdom found Jamaal seated at his desk working so he decided not to disturb him. Entering the gym he found Hakim, Man- Man and Dank preparing to begin their workout.

"Wisdom, thought you weren't going to show up." said Hakim.

"Yea, right." replied Wisdom stretching.

"Did you hear about Mayor Brown dropping out of the race?" Dank asked him

"No, real talk?" Wisdom replies truly surprised.

"Yea, we thought it was your doing." stated Man-Man not putting anything past Wisdom.

"Not me." replied Wisdom while Hakim sat not revealing what he knew.

****

Jamaal spotted Wisdom walking by but wanted to finish up what he was doing before joining them. Before he could stand and stretch there was a knock on his open door.

KNOCK KNOCK

"Come in." said Jamaal.

"Is Wisdom here?" asked the older of the boys

"Who are you?" asked Jamaal.

"Mike, these are my brothers Marco and Melvin."

"Is Wisdom expecting you?" Jamaal asked him.

"You ask a lot of questions." said Marco as Mike grabbed his arm.

Jamaal shot him a mug.

"He told us to come by and he would help us." Mike informed Jamaal.

"Follow me." said Jamaal still mugging Marco.

Jamaal led them down the hall and made a right entering the gym with the boys in tow. Wisdom, Man-Man, Hakim and Dank were rotating from the pull-up bar, dips, and push-ups stopping when they spotted the boys.

"They said you said that you would help them but they didn't say with what." said Jamaal speaking to Wisdom.

"He did." said Marco looking at Jamaal.

"I did, how I can help you?" asked Wisdom walking over to them.

"Can we talk somewhere in private?" asked Mike feeling uncomfortable with so many people around him that he didn't know.

"Were all family in here, you can speak freely." said Wisdom as he watches Mike ponder his options.

"We want to stop hustling and go to school but we can't" said Mike as Marco kicked him.

"Hey, what's your problem?" Jamaal asked getting Marco's attention.

"Our mother told us never air our dirty laundry out in the streets." Marco spat.

"She's right, but we are here to help. Where is

your mother?" asked Wisdom.

"Locked up for possession." Replied Mike.

"What's her name?" Wisdom inquires

"Mona Parks." Answered Mike.

"Where are you staying? Asked Man-Man who didn't receive an answer.

"You got to talk to us if you want us to help you." Wisdom told them.

"We were staying in our apartment until they found out our mother was locked up. Someone called the police but we got away before they could catch us. I started hustling so we could rent a room at the Springdale Hotel each night and have something to eat" answered Mike.

"The division of family services is probably looking for them." Jamaal said.

"Your probably right, are you guys hungry?" asked Wisdom.

"Hell yea" answered Melvin the youngest causing every one to laugh.

"What's so damn funny, I'm hungry." said Melvin not getting the joke.

"Calm down little man. Jamaal will you please take them to the dinning room. Have Sky or Pam make them something to eat while we try to come up with a solution." requested Wisdom.

"No problem, follow me." instructed Jamaal leading the way.

"What you want to do?" asked Man-Man as he watched Hakim get back to doing his pull-ups."

"I want you and Big Hands to get a house together for them to live in if you don't already have one."

"They can't live their alone." Hakim reminds Wisdom.

"I know call Rockford, have him post their mother's bond immediately. Also tell him to work something out with the division of Family Services so they don't take the kids. Then go pick her up and bring her here. Said Wisdom.

"Are we going to bond everyone that gets in trouble?" Hakim asked frustrated.

"Hakim, we will never place money over someone's life. Those boys need their mother and we will help them. She can start classes today part time and work here part time until she gets on her feet." said Wisdom ending the conversation and heading to the shower.

"What's up with you?" Dank said mugging Hakim.

"What?" asked hakim innocently.

"You acting like you've forgotten where you come from and who helped you." stated dank before walking off headed to the shower followed by Man-Man.

Hakim sat down and began reflecting on the entire conversation never noticing Uncle Ronnie enter the room.

"What's wrong with you?" Uncle Ronnie asked him.

"Nothing." replied Hakim.

'I won't ask you again." stated Uncle Ronnie

looking down at him.

"Wisdom and Dank think that I'm being selfish and think that I've forgotten where I came from and who helped me." stated Hakim looking up at him.

"Have you?" asked Uncle Ronnie watching as Hakim considered the question.

"I have been a little selfish but never to family but I've never forgot where I come from or who helped me." stated Hakim.

"There in lies the problem Hakim. We are all family, this entire neighborhood and there is no other way to look at it. We should want for others what we want for ourselves, never forget that." said Uncle Ronnie extending his hand to help Hakim up.

"Yes sir, you are right, I'm sorry."

"Don't tell me, go tell your brothers." said Uncle Ronnie as he watched Hakim walk off towards the locker room.

CHAPTER SIXTEEN

Sleep eluded Richard since he heard Mayor Brown dropped out of the race and left town. With no one else running, he'd won by default. He'd tossed and turn all night thinking about the tough decisions that lay ahead. He knew that there would be some who would take his decision to make replacements of City Officials badly; however, a changing of the old guards is necessary.

Richard dreamed of being Mayor since he was a kid playing in Kinloch Park. He'd dreamed of the day he would have the power to make a change, a real difference in the community. Those in charge had become stagnated and complacent. Combined with their lack of education in economics and business their best efforts just didn't meet the needs of the people who so badly needed them, he observed.

Arriving early at City Hall, Mayor Payne is greeted as he strolled through the halls headed for his first official meeting. Entering the conference room he could feel the tension in the air and immediately notices those who failed to make eye contact with him.

"Good morning, I would like to thank all of you for coming. Today marks the beginning of a new day and era for the City of Kinloch. We've been left behind in an ever evolving world, with us being the equivalent of a third world country. Finger pointing does us no good; we can't un-ring the bells of the past. Some of you have held the same position for years, since I was a kid. Your services have not gone unnoticed or unappreciated." said Mayor Payne looking around the room.

"If you are firing us, let's get this over with." said Georgia Smith an Alderwomen.

"Mrs. Smith, everyone here is a part of the community, a needed part." said Mayor Payne disregarding her comment trying to keep the meeting under control.

"So where do we fit in?" asks Tom Wilson an Aldermen not liking were this was headed.

"Management at City Hall is undergoing a reconstruction, no more good ole boys club or nepotism. Chief Boxer will hand each one of you an envelope with your name on it that holds the key to your future. You have the option of opening it risking that all of the contents become public records or you can hand it back to Chief Boxer. Handing it back is not an admission of guilt; however, if you do so I will expect your immediate resignation. You will stay on as consultants until a full transition is made, then you will move on." stated Mayor Payne as Chief Boxer passed out the envelopes.

"What will happen to the contents of the envelope?' ask Georgia Smith obviously concerned.

"They will be buried in the graveyard of the forgotten past." answered the Mayor.

Each sat contemplating their decision and the Mayors waits. One by one each returned their envelope to Chief Boxer.

"You all are excused from the meeting. I want your resignation on my desk before you leave today." Mayor Payne told them.

Ashley Scott and Walter Evans were the only two still seated looking at the envelope. At the same time both of them opened their envelope, each finding a stack of blank typing paper.

"Welcome to the team. I'm interviewing potential candidates to temporarily fill the others positions. Our first order of business is to stop the drug traffic! Chief do you have a plan?" asked Mayor Payne still observing their expressions.

"Mr. Mayor, we can't stop it." the Chief was saying as the Mayor cut him off.

"That's not the correct answer, maybe I hired the wrong person for the job." stated the Mayor locking eyes with the Chief.

"With all due respect Mr. Mayor, as long as there is a demand for illegal drugs, there will be a black market to supply it. I have a plan that will reduce crime but all of us need to be on the same page." Chief Boxer explains who didn't believe in unrealistic expectations.

"What is your plan?" the Mayor asks.

Chief Boxer explained the unconventional plan that he'd read about that lowered crime by 80 percent across the board in another State. He knew that he would have to convince them to be open minded in order for this to be a success.

"Do you think it will work?" the Mayor ask Ms. Scott,

"I think it could." she replied.

"What's your position?" The Mayor asks Mr. Evans.

"I like it." he replied.

"Then it's a go! Start immediately. Let me know if you need anything, I mean anything that will help you get this accomplished." said the Mayor standing indicating that the meeting was over.

CHAPTER SEVENTEEN

Tyrone and Senator Johnson had moved on to other developers forgetting about Jamaal and his development. Business was good for them, there was always someone wanting to develop something which in turn guaranteed a payday for them.

Both were living the American dream with promising political careers which allowed each to wet their beaks with little to no repercussions.

Today was no exception; they were having lunch on the sixteenth hole at Green Haven, an exclusive Country Club in St. Louis County discussing business.

"Any new clients?" ask Senator Johnson before taking a bit of his steak.

"I'm screening several as we speak" replied Tyrone stopping to look up at him.

"Tell me about them." said Senator Johnson setting down his utensils.

"There is a group of developers trying to build a Board Walk down by the river front like Coney Island. Another developer wants to recreate the French Quarters on a piece of land on Kings Highway. Finally there's a guy who wants to develop land in Cool Valley into a recycling and manufacturing center." said Tyrone taking a bite of his club sandwich.

"Interesting, how much money do we stand to make?" asked Senator Johnson.

"About a million." replied Tyrone.

"What is the hold up? Ask Senator Johnson sipping his wine.

"I'm still looking into their background and finances." answered Tyrone.

'Good, be smart." The Senator was saying as Jamaal and Wisdom approached their table.

"Gentlemen, we hate to interrupt your lunch; however, we have some business that we need to discuss that couldn't wait," said Jamaal taking a seat with Wisdom doing the same.

"Tyrone do you know these gentleman?" the Senator asks feeling a bit uncomfortable.

"We're the gentlemen who gave you $50,000 and Tyrone $100,000 to approve our development in the city of Kinloch." said Jamaal to refresh his recollection.

"Sir, I don't know what your talking about." said the Senator standing to leave.

"Sit your frail ass down unless you want everyone in here to see this!" said Wisdom producing a laptop with a video of the Senator accepting a bag from Tyrone containing the cash they'd given him at a restaurant in Clayton.

Sitting back down the Senator shot Tyrone a mug that could kill.

"That doesn't prove anything." Said the Senator not fazed by what he saw.

"You're an arrogant old bastard but I'll overlook it for now. We kept all of the serial numbers from all of the bills that were given to you by us. We know you placed the money into your daughter's bank account and the rest is in a safety deposit box at Union bank." Said Wisdom as he watches the Senator slump down in his chair.

"What do you want?" he asked knowing that the ball was in their court.

"You catch on quick. I like that. The way I see it you owe us $150,000 dollars, you now work for us." Said Wisdom.

"Now you look here, you got what you paid for." The Senator was saying when Wisdom waived him off.

"You need to calm down before you give yourself a heart attack. You underestimated us thinking that you were dealing a bunch of uneducated people. I knew from the beginning that the approval of the site was not necessary because it had been designated as a center. Tyrone guided by you led Jamaal to believe that obtaining approval would be problematic and that you had the power to expedite the process." Said Wisdom looking directly at the Senator.

"So why did you pay the money?" Tyrone asks dumbfounded.

"Because he wanted to have a chip in the big game." answered the Senator who was used to such a tactic himself.

Wisdom smiles at him.

"What do you want?:" asks the Senator eyeing Wisdom.

"You now work for the campaign to free Kareem Smith." said Wisdom standing.

"And if I refuse, you're going to send us to prison?" asked the Senator testing the waters.

"No, there are things far worse than prison." Wisdom replied smiling wickedly.

"I am a Senator, you're not stupid enough to harm me." stated Senator Johnson trying to convince himself.

"Maybe, maybe not." said Wisdom before leaning down whispering something into Senator Johnson's ear that no one else could here causing him to become pale.

'I'll see what I can do." replied the Senator weakly.

"That would be wise. Gentleman, have a nice day." Said Wisdom patting the Senator on his back as he and Jamaal walked off.

After several minutes and two glasses of wine the Senator got himself together enough at any rate to deal with the situation at hand.

"You gave me $50,000. Where is the rest of my damn money?" the Senator asked Tyrone staring at him.

"They are lying." said Tyrone in his defense.

"Don't fuck with me, get me my money and everything you can on Kareem Smith!" said the Senator standing to leave.

"You're going to help them?" Tyrone asked surprised having never seen the Senator bow- down to anyone.

"Do as I ask." Replied the Senator tired of the questions.

"What did he say to spook you?" Tyrone asked him.

Leaning down with his hands on the table, through clenched teeth the Senator said "He knew that you were my illegitimate son." before walking off.

CHAPTER EIGHTEEN

Phase two is running behind schedule because of the weather and wouldn't be completely finished for at least three months. Rain and Dank were ready to get started and decided to use part of KOFUAA's new facility until phase two is completed.

Over the past couple of months they meet with business leaders, City and County Officials, and potential enrollees for the new program. It had been exhausting work but well worth it.

"Good afternoon, we would like to thank all of you for coming. If Kinloch is going to be the entrepreneurial center of St. Louis, all of us in the community are going to need to help others start businesses. All of you have been chosen for the High Growth Ventures course that simulates planning and securing capital for a startup with the potential to achieve $20 million in annual sales after five years. The 24 of you chosen for this course will be divided into six management teams. Each team will choose one of six preselected innovations, by KOFUAA, as the basis for your startup. Each team needs a CEO, a chief financial officer, a VP of marketing and a VP of operations. Over the semester, we will coach the teams on how to write a business plan, and ultimately pitch your venture. Any questions so far?" asked Dank.

Seeing no hands, he moved on.

"After completing the course you may participate in our first small business program. We are launching a small-business incubator called Teach One, which will provide counseling, networking and other assistance. Our team of business veterans will offer services to your startups in return for a small piece of equity. Teach One will connect you with accountants, bankers, insurance companies and other service providers while helping you avoid pitfalls. Is there anyone who does not want to participate?" ask Dank,

Not receiving a response he continues.

"Good, I'll let Rain have the floor now." said Dank taking his seat.

"Before starting I want to set down some rules for this program: There are only two directions you can go; up or out. We won't tolerate any office politics or snitching to me or anyone else about anything that goes on here; only official complaints will be heard. Second, the only way to advance is to push the person ahead of you higher up the ladder and pull up the person behind you. That way you have a friend on top pulling and a friend below pushing. Any attempt to get promoted by any other means will be result in being kicked out of the program with everyone present to witness it. Finally if you have any problems you think we can help you with, we'll be glad to try and, of course, everything will be in the strictest confidence." said Rain pausing allowing his words to sink in.

"There are two essentials in business: A connection and outlet. A connection will ensure that the price is right so that you can have a competitive advantage and that the product is the very best. With the proper outlet you will be in a position to safely get your product to market. In business it pays to have a link to the resources you need to keep your business thriving and growing: Without the proper connections you are sure to be restricted in your hustle. If either component is missing you will be nothing more than normal. I know it may sound like I'm describing the drug game but I'm not. The only difference between legal hustling and illegal hustling is that those who hustle legally pay taxes. Both need a product, good marketing and reliable customers." said Rain stopping to make sure that every one was following.

"Our plan is rather simple. We will create jobs that produce products that we need, then purchase from ourselves. The tax dollars will be used to build school, add more jobs, and programs." Rain informed them before taking his seat.

"Please feel free to look around and ask questions. There are several business leaders present as well as the Mayor. We are interested in your ideas." said Dank as he watched people begin to mingle.

"What do you think?" asked Rain

"This will be a success." Stated Dank already envisioning its success.

****

For the past two months, Chief Boxer's men had been conducting surveillance on several of the crews doing hand-to-hand. It was rather sad he thought as he watched them. Nothing had changed since he was a kid playing in these same streets except the dealers were more careless. They made his job all the more easier. He was able to track them through the use of their cell phones; GPS in their car, one guy even advertised is product

115

on Craigslist. Carelessness led to more arrests which led to more opportunities to create confidential informants so his cases against them were becoming even stronger.

As a kid it bothered him that no one really cared what happened to the guys after they got locked up. Seemed like people were just happy to be rid of them not realizing that they were pawns in a loosing game, there had to be a better way, this he knew.

"Chief, are you ready to do this?" asked Deputy Smith snapping the Chief out of his thoughts.

"Yes, on my order." said Chief Boxer saying a silent prayer.

"Team one and two, are all of the escape routes closed off?" asked Chief Boxer.

"Yes" replied team one captain.

"Yes" replied team one captain.

"On three everyone move in. ONE, TWO, THREE!" said Chief Boxer.

Several Kinloch Police cars and the paddy wagon came to a stop on the set, no one attempted to run. They thought they had it all figured out never keeping cash, drugs or guns in their possession. Runners accepted the money from customers, weave between buildings so no one can see them, or so they thought, retrieve the product returning it to the customer.

"Lil Nate, I heard you were the new Chief of Police." said Lil Bo who grew up with the Chief.

"It's Chief Boxer and you heard right." replied the Chief.

"What seems to be the problem?" asked Lil Bo

"Your operation and illegal pharmacy." replied Chief Boxer.

"You got the wrong person." Lil Bo tried to convince him.

"Don't think so, turn around." ordered the Chief.

"What are the charges?" ask Lil Bo.

"Depends on your level of understanding, be patient, well get to that." The Chief assured him.

"I want my lawyer." said Lil Bo not liking that answer.

"That's your right, now turn around." stated Chief Boxer placing the handcuffs on Lil Bo then putting him into the back of the police car.

Instead of taking them to the Kinloch jail, they were taken to KOFUAA's new gymnasium searched the un- cuffed. You would have thought this was a family reunion the way they greeted one another, giving hugs and daps.

"Gentleman, please take your seats." yelled Chief Boxer standing at the podium over the loud speaker which didn't seem to get their attention.

"Play the tape." said Mayor Payne.

As the tape began to play on the projector the gymnasium got quiet as every one began to take their seats focusing on what was on the screen.

"As you can see we have all of you dead to the right on multiple drug and weapon charges." Chief Boxer informed them.

"Ain't that about a bitch!" said Ray-Ray standing not believing his luck, he had just got out of prison.

"Youngman have a seat." Instructed Mayor Payne. Ray-Ray complied.

"We understand that we were all raised in an environment where drugs were prevalent and appeared to be the only way out. We recognize that had you been raised around doctors and lawyers then that's what you would have become. Instead you saw a drug dealer who you imitated but that is no excuse." Said Chief Boxer taking his seat as Mayor Payne took the podium.

"Today all of you are being offered a chance at redemption. You will not be prosecuted, all of the evidence that we have collected against you will go into a safe." Mayor Payne was saying before being interrupted.

"I'll take my lumps, I'm not ratting on nobody." said Pat standing.

"That's honorable but we are not asking you to rat on anyone. You see ratting is a big part of the problem so we are implementing a no snitching policy of our own. If you get caught there will be no deals, no one to rat on, we don't want to hear nothing! You will receive what the Constitution guarantees you, a trial by a jury of your peers. I've noticed that the guys who rat are the main problem. They rat on someone, get off easy and are back at it again until they get caught up and then they rat again, not anymore." said Mayor Payne letting his words sink in.

"So what is going to happen?" someone yelled.

"All of you will start classes at KOFFUA today." the Mayor replied.

"Today?" someone yelled.

"Yes, there's no better time then the present time. For those of you who think that you are slick, please let me explain the law to you as it stands. First there is a 7 years statute of limitation on drugs and weapons charges. Second, most of you are ex-felons in possession of a firearm which carries a pretty long mandatory minimum prison sentence. The option is yours go to school or a 6-by-6 wearing jail strips." said Mayor Payne as one of the guys stood up and began to walk off.

"Sir, where are you going?" Mayor Payne asks him.

"Too class, I was rehabilitated once I saw my face on the screen.' said Spook.

"Sir, do you understand that what we are doing is unconventional and a blessing for you?" ask Mayor Payne.

"Yes, I do. I've been to prison, did 6 years and vowed to never go back. When I got out I had a job but got laid off and went back to what I knew best, hustling. Today when those handcuffs were placed onto my wrist, my past flashed before my eyes. I saw myself back in that cage, with guards treating me like shit, having to ask someone to send me money, all the things that I vowed too never let happen to me again." said Spook

"If you are smart, you will take this olive branch that has been extended to you and capitalize on it. KOFFUA will show you how to take the skills that you have and use them in a constructive way, don't mess this up." said Mayor Payne.

"I won't" said Spook walking to the table in the back of the room to sign up for classes.

"Gentlemen and ladies, the past is history, the future if you keep selling drugs and doing wrong is death or prison, so I suggest that you focus on the present, make a good choice today for yourself, your families and this community. Make no mistake, regardless of your decision the City of Kinloch will prosper with or without you. We would prefer that you be a part of this, please make the right decision." said Mayor Payne walking off as Uncle Ronnie took the podium.

"I'm going to say what they can't because it's not politically correct. You all are running around here hustling and still have nothing. If air cost money most of you would be dead, while the rest of you would be trying to put air in your momma's name. You cause all types of problems, and than when someone murders you your mother will have to go into debt trying to bury your sorry ass. Consider yourself double blessed today, not only for the opportunity that is being offered to you today but because I recommended that we water board each of you first but they got to talking about the Constitution wouldn't allow it." said Uncle Ronnie as the Chief stood walking over to Uncle Ronnie who walk off mumbling something.

"Reverend Times, would you like to say something?" ask Chief Boxer

"No, I don't think I could add anything to what I've just heard." he replied.

"Okay then all of you have had time to think about your options, lets get this moving along this is rather simple sign up or get locked up. Sign up on the left, get locked up on the right." said Chief Boxer causing a stampede as everyone rushed to sign up for classes.

Jamaal, Wisdom and Rain stood out of view watching as everything unfolded not believing what they had just witnessed.

"Were you aware of that?" Wisdom ask Jamaal.

"No, I thought you orchestrated it," said Jamaal impressed.

"Naw, I'm just as shocked, didn't see that coming." Said Wisdom.

"It's a great thing." said Rain moved by the entire event.

CHAPTER NINETEEN

Wisdom stood in awe looking around amazed yet humbled by all of their accomplishments. Today was a proud day, one that marked a milestone that some thought that they would never achieve: graduation day.

KOFUAA has been doing great having surpassed 500 students. The school has grown by leaps and bounds since it's founding; pushing its brand through innovative online and social media marketing, In December 2013, the school received $3.1 million in donations to expand the program.

Life couldn't have been better, with phase two completed; phase three was scheduled to begin in a few weeks. Tina, Jackie, and Mona will be the first recipients of the housing program. Shawn, Spooky, Lil Bo and Monna's boys have all signed up as volunteers assisting in the building process.

Mayor Payne and Chief Boxer stood listening as George explained how the homes would be constructed and were really impressed.

"These homes will have basements as foundations, which supports the house, provides stability; exterior walls, interior partitions, which may or may not be part of the primary structure; environmental-control systems, including the heating, ventilating, air-conditioning, lighting, acoustical systems. telephone-wiring systems, the power, water supply, and waste disposal systems." explained George the General Contractor

"We did it babe." Sky said sporting a baby bump Into Wisdom's ear.

"We did." replied Wisdom rubbing her belly.

"Look who I found." said Rain with Jane on his arm. Brinks strolled up behind them with Justice on his arm.

"What, how, you know what, never mind." said Sky hugging Brinks as everyone burst out laughing.

"Ah shit, we back dipping again." said Man-Man as he and Big Hands approached accompanied by Pam and Janet.

"So this is the infamous Brinks that we've been hearing so much about?" ask Janet.

"It is." answered Jamaal walking in on the conversation.

"You all having a meeting without us?" asked Hakim walking in on the gathering as he and Shanna gathered around.

"You must be Hakim?" Brinks asks.

"The one and only, and who might you be?" Hakim wanted to know.

"My grandpa!" Yelled Justice causing Hakim's eyes to widen.

"I'm Dank?" said Dank with Lisa on his arm extending his hand to Brinks.

"Nice to finally meet both of you, I've heard a lot about you." replied Brinks.

"What's going on over here?" asked Uncle Ronnie joining them. Seeing Brinks made him stop dead in his tracks.

"Hi, Pops." Said Brinks

"Don't hi Pops me, get over here and give your father a hug." said Uncle Ronnie.

Brinks quickly made his way to his father embracing him for the first time since he was a child. The moment was emotional for everyone but especially for Wisdom. Seeing the two men he admired and loved so much reconnected was a dream come true for him.

"Pop's, I'm sorry for everything that I took you through." said Brinks into his father's ear.

"There is no need for you to apologize. I should have tried harder to reach you when you fell. I should have been there for you." replied Uncle Ronnie.

"Naw, Pops, what we went through is exactly what we needed to go through, God's plan is never wrong." Said Wisdom releasing his father.

"Every one I need to get going" Jamaal announced.

"Where are you going on graduation day?" asked Wisdom.

"The Mayor and I have a meeting with Mathew Dickey's, Wohls, The Team Center, Herbert Hoover Boys Club, 12 & Park and the Cochran Center in the conference room, were expanding this program." Answered Jamaal smiling and to everyone's delight.

THE END

Good to the Last Drop

18 orgasmic original short stories that are sure to please, this tantalizing page turner is jam packed with over 200 pages that invoke the allure of 50 Shades of Grey combined with the sensuality of Zane to keep you coming back for more.

Pick up your copy today at Amazon.com